Need Me

SHELLEY K. WALL

author of *Text Me* and *Find Me*

CRIMSON
ROMANCE

F+W Media, Inc.

Published by
Crimson Romance
an imprint of F+W Media, Inc.
10151 Carver Road, Suite 200
Blue Ash, OH 45242. U.S.A.
www.crimsonromance.com

ISBN 10: 1-4405-8402-8
ISBN 13: 978-1-4405-8402-2
eISBN 10: 1-4405-8403-6
eISBN 13: 978-1-4405-8403-9

Cover art © iStockphoto.com/ Ysbrand Cosijn.

During the writing of this book, I lost a dear and true friend. He taught me the meaning of strength, loyalty, and perseverance in his nine years with us. He has influenced a canine character in many of my books, this one included, and though his time in my life was short, it will be permanently etched in my soul. Anyone who has had a pet as wonderful as our English mastiff, Conan, can appreciate these words.

Conan stood diligently in our driveway watching the passersby, likely amused at their intimidated reactions. He went on vacation with us, helped our boys meet girls, protected our daughter from harm and our property from intrusion, and gave us many a wonderful dog-hug while drooling all over us. Additionally, he showed our other dogs the right place to pee and how to guard *his* dominion properly.

Two weeks before the final manuscript for this book was submitted, I let him outside to water his normal spots. He strolled behind the foliage in our yard, laid his head over a paw, and slumbered into his next life.

His antics over the years have added a lot of humor and love to our life (see my blog post about his fight with a baby raccoon) and I pray that his time with us was as good as ours with him.

Cheers, Conan.

For my kids…I write romance because there is only one emotion in our life that every single being on the planet seeks, and that is *love*. Yes, it may sound corny, but it's true—and anyone who scoffs at that wisdom is full of crap. May you find it, give it, feel it, and nurture it for the rest of your life.

Lastly, because writing is a frustrating and very solitary profession—I must be thankful for my husband's patience as I waffle from ecstatic celebration to complete despair. Thank you for our life together and your words of wisdom…*it only takes one, you just never know which. So keep writing until you find it.*

Acknowledgments

I must acknowledge Dawn Dowdle of Blue Ridge Literary, who saw a spark in my books and helped bring them to publication. I appreciate her insight and efforts. Additionally I want to recognize my friend Cindy Davis for her editorial advice and friendship during my writing efforts. I also wanted to give a special tribute to Jess Verdi, whose expert eye found many holes in this story. Her advice helped to strengthen the final product and make me fall in love with my characters even more.

My sincere appreciation to Tara, Jess, and Julie at Crimson Romance for their guidance with this series and their continued positive and professional support. They are a wonderful team.

Author's Note

The events in this novel unfold simultaneously with the events of the first two books of this series: *Text Me*, which follows Carter's romance with Abby, and *Find Me*, which follows Jackson's romance with Amanda. This is Caroline and Roger's story.

Chapter One

Six years ago…

Caroline Sanders sat in her silver-bullet gray Land Rover outside frat house row. She loved the way the buildings looked—so clean and perfectly manicured. Sure, the frat boys inside were party animals bent on throwing their parents into financial ruin while they drank, chased girls, and studied-slash-cheated their way to fancy degrees. Tonight was no exception. The red traffic light glared at her while rap music blared from the house to her right. *Geeze, a party on a Thursday night? Don't they have exams like the rest of us?*

She'd just finished one of the many photography gigs that helped pay the bills while she pursued that elusive journalism degree. The traffic light switched to green, but just as she moved her foot to the gas pedal, her passenger door flew open and a bulky frame dropped into her seat. Was she getting *carjacked?*

"Go. Go. Come on, the light's green." The panicked student-looking carjacker shoved the dash as if to propel them forward.

Caroline didn't budge. She took in the wavy, brown hair that fell over chocolate eyes, the dimpled face that gave away a propensity to laugh regardless of his current fear. He didn't *look* like a criminal. His clothes were clean, though tattered, and he held a can of something in his hand. Not beer. She glanced at his gold fingers. Spray paint?

She lifted a brow then looked behind him. On the trunk of the tree in the front yard of the beautiful house was a haphazard drawing in gold—of a kid whizzing on the tree. How childish. "You did *not* just do that. What are you, twelve?"

Footsteps thundered toward the car. "You'd better hit the gas unless you want to get blamed, too." The guy reached a foot over the console and slammed his flip-flop-clad toes over hers.

Against her will, she sped through the light. He kept his foot in place. No chance of turning at the current speed. Another green light accommodated their escape.

A quick glance in the rearview mirror showed half a dozen preppies standing in the street watching their taillights. Gulp. They probably had memorized her plate number.

"You realize you just made me an accomplice to whatever happened back there. Please tell me I won't be tracked down for vandalism."

The guy gave her a quick preview of the dimpled smile he probably used frequently. "Don't worry, I painted over your license plate before I got in the car. You're safe."

Oh, that's comforting.

He returned his leg to the passenger seat and glanced out the window. "You can pull over up there and drop me off. My house is a couple blocks away."

Caroline shook her head. "No way. You jump in my car after doing…whatever you did back there…and my car is probably the only thing all those guys remember. Plus there's gold paint on my license plate that just happens to match the crime scene—"

"There's no crime…or at least nothing serious. You've read too many spy novels. That was payback. Besides, they won't report anything because they don't want us to report *them*." He rolled the window down. As they passed the lake in front of the student union, he flung the can out hard. *Splash.*

"Yes, and you just tossed the only thing that linked *you* to the artwork you left behind. Now my gold-enhanced license plate makes things even worse. No sir, I am not taking you all the way home so I know where you live if someone comes after me. Better yet, why don't I just circle around and drop you right back where I found you?"

The dimples went still. "You wouldn't do that, would you? They'd beat both of us into oblivion."

She gave him a look of intimidation. "Not me. I'd just tell the truth. You, on the other hand, would be in deep shit."

His Adam's apple lunged. Was her ruse working? He sighed. "Something tells me you'd get a kick out of that—watching me get schooled." He closed the window.

Using her best crazy eyes, she nodded. "You have no idea."

"Okay, turn up there." He pointed at a stop sign.

Caroline listened as the guy gave her directions to his home— which wasn't really a home. It was another frat house. Great. He'd pulled her into some sort of fraternity rivalry. It was her senior year, and she'd managed to get this far without any huge explosion. Now this.

"You live here? Seriously?"

"No. I live off campus, but I'm a member. I figured you'd want to know what it was all about. Come on." He stepped out of the car and slammed the door.

Should she follow? Part of her wanted to just hit the gas and leave. *Remember the gold paint on your car?* He should at least clean up his mess. He was halfway up the drive by now, but Caroline remained in the car. "Why should I follow you into that den of sweaty socks and dried beer?" she called out the open window.

He'd kicked off his flip-flops and was now barefoot. He shoved his hands into the pocket of his jeans, which cupped his lower body lovingly, and plodded across the thick grass. "Because you're curious," he called back. "You're dying to know what they did to us. Why else would we want to paint cartoons of little boys pissing on their trees and mooning them on their windows, or fill their vending machines with K-Y Jelly?"

He had a point. Wait, he'd painted little boys baring their asses on the windows? She hadn't seen *that*. "Okay. You're right. I'm curious." She ignored the lubricant comment because that was just plain gross. With a turn of the wrist, she killed the engine and pulled out her keys. She shoved the driver's door shut and plodded toward him. "Aren't you worried you'll stub a toe or step on some glass?"

He grinned. Damn those dimples. They made him look like a devilish preteen prankster, naïve and on the verge of manhood. His looks obviously were deceiving, since he had to be her age. "The lawn crew cuts the grass on Mondays, so it's extra thick by the weekend. I like the way it feels on my toes."

He acted like a preteen too. He reached for her, beckoning with a single finger—and those dimples. Totally wicked. She followed him through the building and into a grassy expanse of yard, complete with pool and spa. Beyond were…tennis courts? *So, this is how the rich kids live.*

The yard was perfectly landscaped, hedges trimmed, grass low and firm. Three smallish trees stood near their path. Oddly, they were already covered, although winter was over a month away.

"See?" He pointed toward the trees.

Caroline shook her head. "No."

"The trees."

She crossed her arms and stepped toward them. Several boxes were scattered at the roots, and the tree covering was wrapped around top and clung down the trunk, like a—condom. *Oh. Funny.* The tree condoms came complete with the word Trojan painted on the fabric.

"Well, it's certainly creative." She clamped her lips tight.

"You think it's funny." Two guys stepped into the grass with beers, and he nodded their way. "She thinks it's funny."

The shorter of the two shrugged and cracked his knuckles against his chin. "It is."

Caroline giggled. "I don't see what the big deal is. Just take it off."

He pointed over her shoulder. "You mean like we did on those two?"

Caroline rotated and dropped her mouth. The two trees he referred to were trimmed like the top of a guy's privates. The shrubs below had been trimmed to resemble the balls. She stuffed a hand over her mouth to keep from spewing laughter.

He rolled his eyes. "We're supposed to have a party this weekend with the Zetas. Not a very classy way to make a good impression."

It wasn't the right time to debate whether frat guys really cared about classy impressions or not. She sucked in air and calmed herself. "Well, it's immature I guess, but hey, so is spray-painting little peeing cartoon figures on their trees. And I won't *even* comment on the lubricant supply. Besides, all you need to do is throw a sheet or something else over them and call it good."

He shook his head. "You really don't get it."

That's right, she didn't. Nor did she care. She needed to get home and go to sleep because she had an exam at nine. *She* was a serious student. "Doesn't matter. I have to leave."

He followed her to the car and stopped when Caroline circled to unlock the door.

"Hey," she leaned over the top, "I want you to clean this damn paint off my car. You do that, and I'll leave things alone. I'm about to graduate, and the last thing I need is trouble. Okay?"

He jogged around the car and held out a hand to shake on their agreement. "You've got it. Where do you live? I'll come pick up the car tomorrow, and we'll detail it and everything."

Right. "Oh no you don't. I've seen your creative skills. I just want the paint removed so I don't get accused of being a part of your prank. The rest of my car can stay as-is."

She pulled a paper from her backpack, wrote down her name and address, gave it to him, and left. Hopefully the other fraternity wouldn't report the paint prank to the police. She'd be able to make it one night with a gold license plate.

At her apartment, she unlocked the door and tiptoed past her roommate, Lyra, who was asleep with the current love of her life on the couch. The girl changed boyfriends like Caroline switched camera lenses.

Caroline crawled into bed. "Oh, *crap*." She slammed a palm to her head.

"What?" Lyra blurted sleepily from the other room.

"I don't even know his name."

"Who?" The voice was closer. At the bedroom door.

Caroline yawned and rolled to her side. "The guy I was with tonight." She let her eyes fall closed.

Lyra giggled. "And you say *I'm* bad."

Oops. Caroline didn't bother to correct the misconception. "You are."

Chapter Two

Roger Freeman stood on the balcony of his third-floor apartment and weighed his choices. He could probably bypass the commitment to clean the paint off Caroline's car because he hadn't given his name. She knew what house he belonged to, but that was all. He only went there for social events, so she'd never find him.

He sighed.

It was the wrong thing to do. In reality, he should have stayed home last night. He had worked and studied so much lately that he needed a break. He could just hear his mom saying, "Haven't I taught you better?" Of course, she'd also say that about his artistic painting skills.

Besides Caroline had amazing eyes—wide set with a slight tilt that made her look like some exotic Disney princess. Even more interesting was her fiery wit, which implied a deep-seated intellect and sense of humor. She wasn't like most of the college girls at frat parties, who seemed to be there for the sole purpose of seeking a husband.

A scratching noise caught his attention and he slid the door open. He rubbed the dog's velvety-soft ears. "Hey, Conan. Come on out, buddy." His dog was the main reason he wanted to live off campus—plus the fact that it was impossible to study with all the noise and drama in that festering frat house.

The dog whimpered and leaned against his leg.

"Want to go for a drive, buddy? You can help me wash a car."

The oversized puppy barked once and circled with his tail wagging. The tail wagged and shook like an epileptic bat. Roger had learned early on to clear all clutter from the tables and shelves. Conan's tail swept away, often breaking anything under two feet off the ground. The mastiff mix weighed seventy pounds at six months and stood almost to Roger's crotch.

Ruff.

"Okay, you talked me into it. Let me get the keys."

He pulled the paper from his jeans and checked the name and address. Caroline Sanders. Nice, kind of old-fashioned. He was glad she hadn't shortened it to Carol. No phone number. Smart, too.

Hmmm. "Let's go, bud." He motioned toward the car, and Conan bolted down the steps in a rumbling mass of scratching toenail and pounding paws. He also left a few drool drops on the steps. There was an elevator on the inside hallway of the apartments, but the dog preferred taking the stairs. Besides, Roger had never liked elevators all that much anyway.

Roger lowered the window of his aged Land Rover so Conan could hang his head out and enjoy the ride. Her vehicle had been the reason he chose Caroline. It was almost identical to his except the color. He knew the locks wouldn't click automatically and hoped the passenger side door would open. It had been a good gamble.

When he pulled up to the weathered and ancient cottage-style house, the dog returned his head to the car and glanced at Roger as if to ask, "Here?"

"This is it." Roger open the door, and Conan bound over him into the street. The dog waited while he extricated himself and then followed him to the porch.

Like many off-campus accommodations, the house was in dire need of repair. Grayish paint flecked from the siding, and the rail around the porch missed a few slats. He noted a plethora of pots filled with plants and flowers. Hers?

Conan stuck his nose into a pot and drooled a little doggy fertilizer into the leaves. He flung his head around. The action caused his tail to swish—toward the pots.

Crash. Uh-oh.

"Conan, sit." Roger pointed at the floor. At least the dog had the brains to comply. Roger rushed to pick up the clay remnants and scoop the plant and dirt into his hand. He darted a glance around for another container. Where could he dump the mess?

"I take it you're not one to sneak into a place quietly and unobserved." Caroline leaned against the open door with a hand fisted on her hip. Her light brown hair was drawn on top of her head in a haphazard knot.

"Leave it there; I'll clean up later."

"Sorry." What an idiotic idea to bring the dog. How would he clean the paint from her car and keep Conan corralled at the same time? He hadn't thought it through. "So, are you a cat person?"

Caroline uncrossed her arms and strode to the rebellious mutt. She kneeled to one knee and massaged his ears. That was all it took to win his favor. In return, the lovesick mutt drooled all over her knee and licked her cheek. She laughed. "I like all animals but don't have any. My landlord won't allow even a hamster or fish. My roommate snuck in a cat for a few weeks—he nixed that right away. Your guy is sweet."

Roger relaxed his shoulders. "Clumsy, big, and horse-like—but not sweet. So, maybe you could take him for a walk around the block while I de-paint your car?"

She eyed him warily. "You just said he's a horse. Am I going to be hauled around the street like a cart?"

Roger shook his head. "Nope. He's great on a leash."

"Then why isn't he on one?"

"Because he doesn't need it. I trained him to heel, and he'll stay at my side most of the time."

Disbelief clouded her features as she furrowed her brow. She pointed to the remains of her plant. "I'd believe you except for a small pile of evidence laying there on my porch."

"Okay, so he got a little excited. That doesn't normally happen."

Caroline patted the dog and rose. "I have a backyard. He'll do great there."

Roger nodded. Even better. Then she could stay with him while he did the chore. Once Conan was secured, they went to work on the car. Paint remover took the golden sheen off the license easily. He followed that with the water hose and a soapy sponge.

When they finished, she stepped back and grinned. "Better than new. You hungry?"

Chapter Three

Caroline tucked her toe under a hip. She sat on the bar stool in her kitchen and watched Roger eat. It was a simple grilled cheese sandwich, but he savored it like a rib eye. How could a guy make the simple act of chewing appear to be the greatest event of his life? Based on his expression, you'd think it was better than sex. She wanted to take his picture. Badly. "Do you always eat like that?"

His eyes bugged. "What? Am I making noise?"

She laughed and shook her head. "No. I just can't remember ever seeing someone enjoy their food as much as much as you. It's…cute." She wanted to say sexy, but changed her mind at the last second.

"Cute? Cute is for puppies, kittens, and little kids. Not grown men. Surely you can come up with something better?"

She already had, but he'd never know. She doubted the term *grown man* applied, either, but chose not to argue. She shrugged. "Why do guys hate that description so much? It's meant as a compliment. I hate to break it to you, buddy, but you're—cute."

He frowned with a wad of sandwich in his cheek, and for a second she thought they shared a moment. She concentrated on meeting his gaze, but it wasn't easy. He seemed to take inventory of her features in a way that made her feel small and unworthy.

Roger was comfortable in his skin, more so than most college students ever achieved. He seemed to see right through her, and she was pretty sure he'd already decided to leave as soon as the sandwich was finished. Which it was. He ran his fingers through a sexy mop of thick brown hair and wiped his mouth. At least he used a napkin—aka a paper towel—unlike most guys his age. He wadded the napkin and tossed it toward her trash can. It fell short and bounced across the tile, skidding to a stop under the cabinet. "Oops."

"You need to work on your shot."

"Guess so. I wasn't much on the three-pointer in high school. My shot was taking a jumper from the top of the key." His face lit up with a warm smile. A flitter of nervous anxiety flicked through her body.

Caroline stood and took a breath, sucking it in like a cold drink on a hot day. She was in trouble. Roger's warm brown eyes crinkled into a caramel-colored pool of enticement. The last thing she needed in her senior year was enticement. "Thanks for washing my car. All I really wanted was to get the paint removed, but you went way beyond. It looks amazing—for a ten-year-old Land Rover."

A loud thud interrupted their meeting of the eyes, and Caroline was thankful to have a distraction. Roger lifted his head and peered out at the yard through her back window. "I hate to break it to you, but I think Conan just killed your lawn chair."

Outside, the dog had attempted to curl himself into the seat of her weathered chair. Unfortunately, Conan's weight and four sharp-nailed paws were more than the chair could stand. The fabric had torn so that his back leg hung through to the ground. The hound whimpered and searched for assistance, trying to tug himself free, until the chair wobbled and flipped over on top of him.

Caroline and Roger stood for a moment and watched the spectacle, side by side, hands on hips. She laughed. Testosterone oozed from Roger's pores; she could practically touch it, only inches from her arm. She stepped back, needing to put a little more space between them.

Roger pulled the door open and stepped into the yard. The dog shot him gooey help-me eyes from the depths of the demolished chair. The water hose had saturated his T-shirt to a nice body-clinging fit, and Caroline found it impossible not to stare. He reached up and tugged the sucking fabric free from his abs. It peeled from his back like scorched skin from a sunburn, unwilling to release its hold. Her breath hitched as the sun glanced across his back and highlighted the roundness of his shoulders under the transparency of wet cotton.

She grabbed her camera from the counter and raised it to her eye. Click. Click. Click. He bent over and eased each paw free and walked Conan from the debris of her former sunbathing chair. Click. Click. She should have asked before taking the pictures, but the moment was perfect. This big burly student saving his pet from misery. Epic.

"Sorry about that....I guess I owe you a chair now. And a flower pot. I should have left him at home. He tends to tear things up when he gets excited." The dog planted his ass next to Roger and panted, unconcerned about the fate of the chair. Roger rotated toward Caroline and stopped as he teetered to balance on his bent legs. Click. She snapped one last shot of him squinting through a morning burst of light.

"You're taking pictures."

She shrugged. "Yes, is that okay? He's just such a great animal. I'm a journalism major, and I'm always looking for subjects that appeal to our emotions. He's perfect."

"You're taking pictures of *me*."

Busted. She shrugged. "Um, yeah, *and* the dog."

He strode toward her with a hand outstretched. "Give me the camera."

Uh-oh. Was he mad? Would he delete all the images? She swallowed. "I'm sorry—I should have asked." She handed over the camera.

He grinned and looked at the display, scrolling through each frame. "You're good. I like them."

Caroline shrugged. "I take pictures for events as a side job to pay my rent."

He lifted the camera and pointed her way. Click. He moved to her side. Click. "It's only fair to have you in the frame, too. After all, how can you accurately record something if you're not *there*? Right?"

She nodded and bathed in his smile. *Whatever you say, Mr. Chocolate Eye Candy.* "Right."

"Listen, Caroline, I was wondering…would you be interested in going with me to this party I have to attend next weekend?"

Damn. Did she really want to get involved with a guy who painted cartoons on trees, who obviously hasn't fully matured? She stared into those crinkled eyes.

Oh, what the hell.

• • •

The following weekend, Caroline analyzed the chains laid out on the entry table at the Tau Kappa Epsilon house and cringed. "What are those for, and remind me why I agreed to this?"

She stopped suddenly at the door, and Roger banged into her from behind, sending her forward a step. "What's wrong?" His breath fanned the back of her neck.

Oh, Lord, how long was this fiasco supposed to last? She couldn't help but widen her eyes. "I'm wondering if I should have asked more than just the time and place for this party." She picked one of the chains up and felt his chest warm against her shoulder as he peeked over.

"Oh. Um, yeah, I should have told you the theme. To be honest, I'd forgotten myself. It's a 'ball and chain' party."

"What's a ball and chain party?"

"Don't worry—no one's going to lock you in a dungeon or anything."

That wasn't exactly what had passed through her mind, but it was good to know. No, her thoughts had gone straight into the gutter. A gutter full of chains and ties and him—naked—but she'd never admit those thoughts to a soul.

"We'll be hooked together for the evening," Roger explained. "I go where you go and vice versa. There are little armbands on the end of each chain, see?"

Seriously? Wow. Who came up with that idea?

He stepped past and grabbed her hand, pulling her along. Was he afraid she'd turn and run? She was tempted to plan an escape route and darted a glance around, just in case things went sour. Her thoughts must have been all over her face because he smiled one of his trademark dimpled bolts of happiness.

A tallish guy with brown curls slid their way—reminding her of an old Tom Cruise movie from her mom's day. Except his sneakers squeaked on the tile as he approached. "Hi there, I'm Sean. Are you Roger's date?"

Caroline glanced between the two men. "That depends."

"On what?"

"On whether we're going to do anything crazy and stupid while tied together like prisoners." She lifted her hand to jingle their intended jewelry.

Roger playfully yanked on the ponytail she'd twisted at the back of her head. "Well, it would be a shame to waste all these great toys, right? Sean, this is Caroline. She's a little worried about the chain thing."

Sean grinned. "They're safe. The cuffs are just made out of elastic hair ties, so you can take them off if you guys get sick of each other or something. It's just for fun. We have some games inside, too, and there's a prize for whoever can complete all the games while staying connected for the duration of the evening. Oh, and if he disappoints you, come back and trade him in—I'm sure every guy here would kill for a chance to be handcuffed to you for a night, girl."

Caroline sent her gaze skyward for half a beat, then twisted the elastic band between her fingers and gave it a couple of tugs. "Thank God they're not *really* handcuffs."

Roger rolled the elastic over his hand and winced. "Shit, it's a little tight. Handcuffs might have been a little more comfortable. It feels like my circulation is being cut off."

Sean rolled his eyes. "That's hers, dumbass. There's a big end and a little end. You get the big one."

"Why didn't you say that first?"

Caroline couldn't resist. "Oh, rats. He promised me *I* would get the big one tonight."

Sean's voice resembled a jackhammer as he laughed, and he motioned the people behind them to step forward for their armbands.

Caroline took the smaller band from Roger and rolled it into place. What a novel idea for a party, though she wasn't sure if the intention was to scare people away from making commitments or just give these hormonal idiots a chance to play at bondage. Surely the organizers hadn't actually believed they could build a relationship out of tied together for the evening? The two entered the great room of Roger's frat house, which was decorated with hand-painted signs featuring relationship-bashing smears and ball-and-chain jokes. Well, that eliminated one theory. The environment didn't seem too conducive to a romantic handcuff-induced rendezvous, either. It was bound to be a long evening.

Another guy shoved an unopened beer toward Caroline, and she reached to grab the drink. Roger's arm accompanied hers, whooshing out and hitting her in the side. She grabbed her rib. "Oops, sorry about that—chain hazard," he said.

She shrugged. "No worries."

His breath tickled her ear as he moved his free arm past to signal for a second drink. "I guess I should probably apologize upfront for anything my fingers or arms do without my knowledge based on their bondage level." Another beer appeared, and they both popped the cans open with their free hands.

"Now that's an excuse I haven't heard before." Caroline turned to survey the small crowded room and bumped right into Roger's chest. "Yikes. This is going to take some getting used to."

"Bump into me all you want. I won't complain."

"You say that now, but wait until I spill this all over you. Then you might change your mind."

He shrugged. "The cleanup might be kinda fun. Let's go see what the games require. You ready for this?"

Nope, but if she ditched the chain, would she be whipped for desertion? She wasn't ready for anything so, um, brutal. But that wasn't entirely true—she was nothing if not courageous. She'd craved any form of adventure for years, and her upcoming graduation came with the promise of a new escapade—into reality. Roger lifted his beer and took a sip. Caroline figured she'd better take advantage of his raised glass and do the same.

Roger pointed toward a group. In unison, they shifted their drinks to the other side. She followed with her arm dangling alongside his, their fingers only inches apart. She hoisted their arms up. "They could have at least given us a little more chain. What is this…twelve inches? What if I have to pee?"

Roger lifted a brow but kept his dimples still. "I promise I won't look—at least not much."

She reached up to punch him, but the chain yanked his hand along and she whiffed. Not to be deterred, she put the beer in her chained hand and swatted him with the other. At least he didn't say anything gross about the twelve inches. "I seriously doubt that."

The room had wall-to-ceiling windows, and the thick curtains were drawn to display outside activities. Caroline's eyes popped as she spotted a giant yellow-and-blue jungle gym in the yard. Teams of two slithered through tubes that were barely big enough for one adult male, let alone two people chained together. Gulp.

"That looks like fun," Roger said. She didn't have to look to know his dimples were showing. She gave him a short elbow jab to the stomach, and the chains jingled as if enticing her to deliver more punishment. She debated a second jab and realized it probably wasn't very courteous to abuse her escort.

Roger rubbed the spot on his abs. "You know, we don't have to do this if you don't want to. We can always go get a pizza and beer. Or study at the library. Don't feel like you're committed."

Committed. A funny choice of words, considering the theme of the party. She'd never been one to shy away from a challenge, and today wouldn't be the first. "The library on a weekend night? Are you kidding? This is right up my alley. I love a good time and a good competition. Bring it on, baby." She reached up and grabbed the collar of his shirt, then dragged him in for a short kiss. Hard. Firm. Good tension and just the right amount of challenge.

Roger yanked backward, jangling chains and sloshing beer. "That was unexpected."

She shrugged. "I figured we'd get it out of the way first, considering we're tied to each other for the night. We'll have to rub many more body parts together if we want to win."

Roger's jaw dropped. With false bravado, Caroline strolled forth into the group of people, forcing him to lurch after her. A warm tingle started to rise from the depths of her insides. There was something oddly enjoyable about having the power to make someone follow—and more. She supposed if she itched her nose, his hand would also touch her face. Should she test the theory?

Why not? She lifted her hand, but instead of itching her nose, she pushed her hair back from her face. Oomph.

The rope was longer than thought. His hand connected just below her collarbone. A few more inches and he'd have copped a feel.

He coughed. "You planning to warn me next time you do that, or just slap me after?"

Caroline gave him an innocent blink of her eyes. "You mean I get to choose?"

He lifted the chain. "You're in charge, gorgeous."

"I like the sound of that. So what're the rules of this giant hamster cage? Do we just have to make it through to the end while staying tied up? Or is there more?" From the ground, the challenge appeared bearable, but her cynical nature knew there had to be a catch.

Roger shrugged. "No idea. Let's ask."

Chapter Four

The giant hamster cage was a rented jungle gym that one of Roger's frat brothers had found. The beginning of the obstacle course had rope ladders resembling a ship's net. There were tubes above where Roger and Caroline could vaguely see people flopping and sliding around within, but it was clouded with age.

A hand shot out and slithered down the inside of the tube near the end. Wait. That wasn't age-induced clouding—it was oil. Holy hot-mamma-mud-wrestling, they were expected to oil up and slither through the entire thing. *Gulp*. Roger's face burned so hot that he figured it had to be worse than a hot flash. He shot a glance at Caroline as she focused on the contraption. Based on the way her eyes had narrowed, she also registered the lubrication involved. He expected her to be in full panic mode, ready to cut and run.

Roger swallowed the mass of saliva in his throat. "You know, I'm really hungry. Why don't we skip this and go have a pizza and some beer? We could…"

But he trailed off because her eyes danced back and forth with… excitement. How could she be so unshaken? Caroline wrapped her shackled arm around his neck and pulled him close until her nose was nearly touching his. She jutted her chin seductively and batted her eyelashes. He focused on the way the golden flecks in her pupils sparkled. Challenge lay in their depths. Her words fanned his face with bravado. "I believe you're chickening out. Or maybe you're afraid I will cave? Come on, Mr. Big Talk, let's do this."

The couple in front of them was doused with canola and pushed toward the ropes. They swiped shiny lather from their eyes and reached up with shackled hands.

Roger's arm yanked skyward without his volition as Caroline closed eyes, her head raised and mouth shut, and flung her arms out as if she was about to be nailed to a cross. With that pose, it was easy to admire the shape of her neck and the curve of her breasts beneath her shirt, a red, slinky top with short sleeves. In a couple seconds it would be—

Splash. Ruined.

Roger spit the oil from his mouth. He smelled like a greasy peanut. "Hey, a little warning would have been nice." He rolled his fists over both eyes until it felt safe to open them.

Caroline was attempting the same, which made it easy to take another quick glance at her figure through the wet fabric. With her fingers dripping goo, she blinked three times—her lashes thick with a greasy sheen. She choked out a laugh. "Okay, let's go, Slick. Pun intended." She reached for the rope ladder and his arm jolted after her; Roger had no choice but to climb.

Oil rolled down the inside of his shirt and into the crack of his briefs. *Oh, that feels great.*

Caroline pushed up the ladder with relative ease, considering their feet slipped on most of the rope rungs the first try. He'd better book it if he didn't want to pull them both down. Three rungs up, he glanced below to see a shiny puddle on the ground. Hmmm. If they happened to miss a rung and slide down, he could probably break the fall—but she'd likely slither off him like syrup rolling over a pancake. "You know, this would have been much more fun if they'd used something tasty…like syrup."

Caroline's foot slipped but she caught herself. "And get swarmed by bees or flies? No thank you."

"Watch it Caro—as in Karo syrup."

"Har. Har."

He shoved up beside her to the top of the rope ladder and watched her as she rolled onto the platform above. Her clothes clung to her like cellophane, leaving nothing to the imagination.

Caroline had a nice frame—small, thin, and waif-like. Unlike him. He settled beside her and pointed at the tube beyond. "There's no way we'll fit in there together, no matter how well we're greased up. So who goes first?"

Caroline ran the back of her free hand over her face in a failed attempt to de-grease herself. "I have a feeling if I go first, you'll be staring at my ass all night. So, I vote for you."

He grinned, not because she was right but because he'd already noted the way the polka dots on her bra were visible through the slickened fabric of her shirt. Would the panties match? He shrugged. "So let it be done."

Roger rolled over Caroline, glancing briefly into her eyes and noting the way the light reflected off the sheen of her lips. He wanted to taste them again—regardless of how many people watched.

Someone yelled from below. "Move it along, you two. Save that for later—there are people waiting."

Roger's wet leg slipped between hers. Damn. He felt every slippery inch of that fine waifish body against him. He coughed and crawled into the tube. "Whoops."

"Wait."

Roger looked back.

"Turn around. The chain's not long enough. Go backward, and I'll go forward." She did a little curled movement with the index finger of her free hand.

"Good idea."

He pulled backward, rotated, and wedged himself feet-first into the tube. Crawling backward would be a lesson in agility and self-control. But there was one additional problem. Going backward also involved staring into her slickened face the entire way—or looking past and trying *not* to stare at the lipid curves of her back, hips, or legs. He was screwed.

"By the way, I thought you should know that you're oiled up like a body builder in a world fitness competition. I can see every inch of you."

He grinned. "Funny, I was thinking the same thing about you. So, you're checking me out, are you?"

She put a hand to his face and squeezed his cheek. Her fingers slipped. "Roger, I checked you out when you first dove into my car. You really think I would have driven anywhere with you if I hadn't summed you up and deemed you—"

"Harmless?" He wasn't sure he liked the implication. Did he want her to think he was harmless?

Caroline licked her lips, doing nothing to remove the oil. "That wasn't exactly the word that came to mind, but you didn't appear to be a rapist or a mass-murderer. No."

Roger lumbered backward through the tube, drawing Caroline along, luring her closer. "That's good to know."

She looked over his shoulder. "There's a turn coming up, then a bit of a climb."

He tried to peer over his shoulder. "How the hell am I going to go backward up a ladder?"

"I'll push you."

He leveled his eyes with hers. "Seriously? Look at me. I've got at least a hundred pounds on you. You really think you can push me up that thing with all this extra lubrication? No way. Let's get to the bottom of the ladder, then you crawl under me and we'll climb it together. It looks a little wider there; we can probably fit."

A loud scream pierced their ears, then a mass of giggling. "Wonder what that was all about."

Judging by the laughter, he assumed someone was enjoying this almost as much as him. He shook his head. "No idea. Let's move though or the next group will catch us." There was something intimate about being cooped up in a six-foot space together. He knew there were at least forty other people around them either inside or outside of the maze. But still, this little section was theirs.

Roger back-crawled into the opening of the ladder, keeping his chained arm low, then stood and made space for her to join. Caroline slithered in and palmed the walls as she wedged herself against him. Rising to her feet, her face was inches from his chin. Good thing she was so petite; they'd never fit together otherwise. As it was, they fit perfectly. She looked into his eyes and blinked. God, he liked the way her eyes looked like rounded almonds in the light. She stilled, her mouth parted as if waiting. There was no way he could let the moment pass—it was too perfect. He bent down and passed his mouth lightly over hers, tasting the oil mixed in with her lip gloss. An odd mix of vegetable fat and… strawberries. Unusual, but he liked it. He bit gently against her lower lip and delved in for another taste, longer this time. Deeper. Caroline adjusted her head and opened her lips for him. Seconds ticked by.

"Ahem." Someone coughed. Uh-oh. The couple following them had caught up.

Caroline smiled. "We'd better get moving."

He nodded and held still as she curled around and pressed her back against him. *Gulp*. Roger enclosed her in his arms and legs and they crawled up the ladder together. *Focus on anything else. Anything but the fact that he was oiled to the max and pressed against this delicious little thing who had just kissed his brain cells into orbit.*

His mind was cluttered with too many confusing thoughts to utter a word. Her thighs, cradled against his, rubbed and glided in unison with his movements. Her back fit perfectly into the space between his arms. They climbed to the top in silence. As the tube opened to night air, they looked up to see the flickering stars. To their left, a platform led to a slide. He glanced at the bottom. The slide ended in the pool, where bubbles and puddles of oil coated the top of the sea-green water. He really should have asked more about the party before committing. Neither of them were dressed for a shindig that involved getting this wet and slippery.

"Fresh air." Caroline sucked in a deep breath and he noted the way her chest pressed into him. It was too much.

"Yeah, let's get out of here. I'm dying." *Dying to finish whatever that kiss had started*, he thought. He was a moron, a sex-starved, hormonal idiot—like every other student in his fraternity.

Loud voices rose over the music that blared from speakers nearby. A screaming match had ensued between Nathan Chenton, the president of the fraternity, and his girlfriend. He grabbed her by the arm and marched her to a more private spot below their perch.

The girl whirled to face her date. "Are you kidding me? I am not going in there and ruining this." She ran a hand down her bikini top and matching sarong. Obviously *she* had seen the party agenda and dressed appropriately, so what was the problem?

"Lannie, it's a swimsuit. That's what they're made for: getting wet."

Lannie dropped a hand on her hip and bobbled her head from left to right. "*This* is a three hundred dollar outfit. I am *not* slathering it in frying grease. I thought you were using water."

"We are." He lifted a chained hand and yanked hers up to point at the pool. "Look. We go through the jungle gym and rinse off in the water."

Lannie yanked the chain from her wrist and tossed it toward his chest. "*We* aren't doing anything. I am not ruining my suit or dousing my hair in that mess—I just had it colored this morning. You go ahead without me."

She was cold as an ice cube in her three-hundred-dollar, made-to-be-sexy suit. Not to be deterred, Nathan held up the chain. "Looks like I need a sub, ladies. Anyone interested?"

Lannie slapped his face. "You slither around in there with one of those sluts and I'm gone, asshole."

He shrugged. "Okay, then. Bye." Holding up his hand, he wiggled his fingers until the chain dangled free.

Roger sighed and leaned into Caroline's ear. "In case anything else happens, I just wanted to say thank you."

She met his eyes. "For what? We're not done yet."

"For being a good sport. Not many girls would be willing to do this."

She glanced at the bikini-clad blonde who disappeared through the crowd. "Obviously. Good thing for you I shop at Target and don't dye my hair."

He reached his hand to his chest, yanking hers atop as well, and clutched the oily fabric of his shirt. "Be still my heart! You're perfect."

She laughed and stepped toward the slide. "That's right. No wonder you're falling for me and following me everywhere I go."

Yep, especially with handcuffs involved, he thought. *If only she knew how true that statement could become.* She sat down on the edge, yanked on the chain, and he plopped to her side at the top of the slide. Would she still feel chipper once they were soaked to the skin and freezing without a change of clothes? "Come on, ball, your chain's on the run. Just be glad it's not bikini Twister. I hate that game—so unoriginal."

Uh oh. Obviously she hadn't seen the Twister game at the far corner of the yard. Roger scooted his legs to fit around Caroline and noted how perfectly they melded together within the confines of the waterslide. "So unoriginal. You ready?"

He pushed off before she had a chance to answer. Her laughter was a fresh relief compared to the numerous screams he'd heard earlier. Who was this girl, and where had she been for the first three years of his college life?

Chapter Five

The following morning, Caroline blinked an eye open and stared at the large plastic trophy on the floor beside her bed. Meanwhile, Roger was spooned against her in nothing but a pair of her old roommate's shorts. Her legs rubbed warmly against the hairs on his thighs. She'd offered him a shower after returning to her apartment the night before, and the shorts were the only things she had large enough for him to change into. She'd showered after him and put on shorts and a T-shirt, and somewhere along the line, they'd both fallen exhausted into bed. Fully clothed, of course. She was adventurous but not stupid. Still, her clothes felt too thin at the moment.

The inscription on the trophy was like an omen. It made her nervous.

Most Likely to Stay Chained.

Technically, they'd come in third place. But the judges must have admired their courage—noting she was fully clothed, not in a swimsuit, and hadn't complained—because they voted them winners.

The sunshine glinted off the cheesy trophy. She giggled. Roger had bet her she couldn't keep the wristband on more than an hour once the game ended. She loved a good dare. Apparently he did also because he'd stayed with her, taking his off only for the short minutes during her shower.

"What's funny?" Roger's voice feathered over her shoulder.

She started to sit, up but the chain had lodged over her ribcage, forcing her to wriggle around to face him instead. "All of it. Us, slathered in vegetable oil. You covering me with your shirt to keep the guys from staring at my see-through blouse—"

"You make me sound noble."

"You were." She patted his chest with the chain still attached at the wrist. It was wedged so tightly between them it couldn't jingle. The chain-link indentions on her stomach felt like they could be permanent. She glanced at her clock. Eleven a.m.

Roger ran his other hand over his eyes and squinted at the bright window. "Not really. I'd already done my share of looking; I just wasn't letting the other guys have theirs. That polka dot bra was pretty unnerving."

She glanced down at said bra laid out on the floor. "Glad you liked it."

"Liked it?" he groaned. "I loved it—it makes me want to look through the rest of your underwear."

Hmmm. That sounded interesting—and a little provocative. "I'll bet. You want to wear them, too?"

He snickered. "Whatever makes you happy. I aim to please."

Rearing her head back, Caroline met his melt-me eyes. "Do you now?" She hitched an inviting brow...then panicked. This wasn't like her; she didn't normally jump into bed on the first real date with a guy.

Technically, they weren't really in bed. She noted the softness of her pillow under their joined heads. Okay, they *were* in bed, but there hadn't been any sex involved. Just a hell of a lot of heavy kissing. She tried to focus on his face, but his lips twitched and the dimples caved. He'd found her weak spot. She was a sucker for his boyish—or was it devilish?—smile.

"Wanna test me, Caroline? I'm game if you are."

She patted his collarbone again in admonishment. "I'll bet you are. Would that be with or without the chains? Do you trust me enough to let me go?"

"Your choice, gorgeous."

That sounded like a line he'd used before. Probably many times. "So, um, it's late—or early, depending on how you look at things. And according to my clock, I have to take pictures in an hour."

Roger's grin wavered. "I guess that means no."

She nodded, partly because words were failing her and partly because she really needed to get away from him for a short while. He was too warm. Too solid and hard. Too—everything. Plus she really *did* have to go to work. She'd committed to taking senior pictures for a few students and needed to be on campus. She cleared her throat. "I know it's a heartbreaker not to wear my underclothes, but duty calls."

Roger sat up. The movement pulled the chain from her ribs. She should have felt free, less confined. Instead, a rush of cold remorse swept over her, and she shivered.

"How long will the job last?" he asked.

She shrugged. "A few hours maybe. I'm not sure." Suddenly she wanted to ditch the job. If there were a way to contact the students and cancel, she probably would. But there wasn't. "Um, you want to go with me?"

The dimples returned. "Sure, why not?" He stood and looked down at the girly shorts and knotted his eyebrows. "Maybe I should go home and change, though. Let's meet afterward. Okay?"

Caroline couldn't help but admire the way his hip bones tilted down into the shorts. "I dunno. I kind of like your outfit. Those shorts look so much better on you than they did on Faith. And I can assure you I never ever had the desire to do this with her." She hooked a thumb in the waistband of the shorts and pulled him against her.

His breath gushed out as their chests bumped. She hesitated, hoping he'd bridge the rest of the gap and—

He kissed her.

Yeah, she'd meet him anywhere, anytime. He kissed like he was half-crazy and half-angel. Or maybe it had been way too long since she'd had a decent kiss and she was desperate. His kisses weren't exactly decent—anything but—but they were still addictive. Whatever the reason, who cared?

She strung her fingers into the hair at the nape of his neck. His breath waved hotly over her swollen lips. "See you after, gorgeous," he said. He pulled free and made to leave, but not before he yanked her terrycloth robe over the shorts. With shoulders straight, he strutted away as he knotted the tie around his hips. So cute. And so very funny.

"Back at you, Rog," she said, and he was gone.

A moment later, Caroline's cell rang. She glanced at the screen—it was her mother, Carol. She answered and was drowned in small talk. Fifteen minutes later, she ended the conversation and jumped in the shower.

Amazing how the oil still seemed to find places to hide. She soaped out her ears and armpits, then shampooed her hair for the fifth time. Once satisfied, she dressed, grabbed the camera, and headed for campus. A quick glance at her cell showed a text message from Roger with instructions to meet at the Wing Stop next to campus in a couple hours. She smiled and thumbed an affirmative response.

It was perfect weather for an outdoor photo shoot. Some people are naturally photogenic. Others require a lot of work. Her first two people were tough, not because they weren't attractive. In all honesty, she rarely found anyone who couldn't be attractive in a picture. No, these two seemed to have their minds made up on how the pictures should look. It took a lot of patience and convincing before they'd let *her* call the poses and backgrounds.

"You're good at this." The first girl focused on her silhouette against the backdrop of the student union. The lighting cast dark shadows across her cheeks, enhancing the fullness of her lips. She was a slightly large girl, and the shadows emphasized her beautiful face rather than focusing on her fullness. It was perfect.

"Thanks." Caroline flipped a card over and scribbled down information on the back. "You can view the proofs at this website after ten p.m. tomorrow. I'll need half the cost today, the rest once you choose which package you'd like to have. Also, check out some of the gift items on the website—your parents might like a frame or something." Caroline's first client left happy.

The second girl tried to pose at the onset. It was obvious she was nervous—and that her clothes weren't designer, which was refreshing. She was honored the girl had chosen her—even more so after learning she was the last of five siblings and the only one to graduate. The picture would mean a lot to her parents, and Caroline had to do the job justice.

Caroline handed her a photo book under the guise of choosing a "look," then, while the girl focused, she clicked away, snapping shot after shot. A cap and gown lay in the background waiting for her. The girl's fantastic chestnut hair fell over one shoulder in a gentle blanket of brilliance. After the girl handed the photo book back and explained her preferences, Caroline suggested she walk for a few steps and shot several more frames. Perfect. They added the cap and gown for a few more before reviewing the images.

Another satisfied customer. Once the girl was gone, Caroline tucked the check into her pocket, praying it wouldn't bounce. With most of the students she dealt with, there was a fifty-fifty chance their bank balance wouldn't cover the work. Regardless, there was satisfaction in knowing she'd recorded their special life moments. She labeled the camera's memory stick with the name, date, and file number, then loaded an empty memory stick for the next session. The fall wind caught her hair and tossed it into her eyes. She should have tied it back, but there hadn't been time this morning.

"Well, well. If it isn't polka dot panties," a mocking voice called out from behind her.

She whirled around to face the source of the comment. Uh-oh. It was Roger's frat brother, Nathan—the one dumped by the fancy bathing suit chick.

"Technically, it wasn't panties but a bra. Hi. I'm Caroline." She held out a hand but stepped back a half-step. The guy was in her face.

He snickered. "Details, details. Looked great to me."

Her face flooded with heat. Why was she dying to wipe that smirk to China? Maybe it was the way he'd ran his eyes slowly up and down her body, stopping chest-high as if imaging the bra. She shuddered. "I'm working at the moment, so I can't talk. Maybe you could come back later?"

His gaze floated over her shoulder and focused on something at her back. She forced herself not to look. He squinted. "You're working here?"

"Yes, I'm a photographer. I'm waiting on my next client, a Mr., um…" She glanced at her schedule.

"Nathan Chenton."

She felt her eyes widen. "You?" Oh, *shit*.

He grabbed her forearm, rubbed a thumb along her skin, and winked. "That's me."

Vomit surged into her throat. He winked? Seriously? And what was with the thumb massage? *So* gross and stupid. "Okay, then. Hang on a second while I change my battery. This one's almost dead." Caroline pulled free, turned, and reached into her camera bag.

"I'd like to charge your batteries—just say when."

Heat burned like lava in her cheeks. He did *not* just say that. She peered over her shoulder and saw that he had oddly crouched down. Was he seriously trying to look up her skirt? It was laughable—especially considering it wasn't a skirt but a skort— but he was acting just so…high school. She whirled around and dropped a hand on her hip. So that was how it would be, huh? Okay, no problem. She'd dealt with his type before. She could handle the likes of one smartass spoiled college guy with a giant ego.

"Just curious, um, Nathan, but I lost you after the party the other night. I was so wrapped up—and I mean *wrapped tightly up*—with Roger that I didn't get a chance to seek you out and say how much I enjoyed the whole thing. What a great idea for a party."

He blinked, clearly not sure if she was issuing a compliment or insult. Good, she had him confused. She lifted the camera and clicked. He stuck his hands in his pockets. "Hey, I wasn't ready."

She put on her sweetest smile. "That makes two of us then. You snuck up on me, and I snuck up on you. Imagine that. So…about that battery charging thing." She kept the camera plastered to her face and watched.

He dropped the swagger for a second and stared into the distance. *Click. Click. Click.* "Don't I get a warning or something? Can't I at least smile for you?"

She shrugged. "Why? A smile is so…" She bit her lip before the word *phony* slipped from her mouth. "Predictable." She dropped the camera and tossed her hair from her eyes. The wind kindly whipped it back. "You know," she said, "you could be one of those male models. Have you ever thought of doing that?"

Sure, it was about as full of shit as a cow pasture, but it worked. He dropped the swagger and gave her a normal smile, not one of his hey-come-bed-me faces. *Click. Click.*

But then his face went sober. With two steps her way, Nathan reached for the camera. "I don't like the way this is going. Can we just talk for a few minutes? Put that down."

Caroline jolted backward and tripped over her bag. She held her hands up to save the camera, but she fell flat on her ass. *Ouch.* That would leave a bruise. "Don't touch my equipment please."

He reached for her arm. "I wasn't going to touch your… equipment. Or anything else. I just wanted to talk. I thought maybe we could go get a drink or something."

What? Wait a minute. Had he seriously thought she'd go out with him after taking the shots?

"Nathan, what the hell are you doing here?" Roger's voice rang out in the distance.

Nathan dropped Caroline's arm and lurched around. "Oh, hey man. I'm getting my senior pictures taken. She…fell."

Roger sidestepped around Nathan and reached out a hand. "You okay, gorgeous?" He waited with fingers extended as Caroline surveyed the situation. Part of her was worried that he had decided to check up on her at work. But she was amused that he'd interceded when Nathan knocked her over. Was he jealous?

She met his eyes, noting the way they darkened to deep ebony. *Oh, my God, he is.*

She grabbed his hand and lurched to her feet, then wiped the grass from her skort. "I'm great. I thought we were meeting later." Somewhat relieved to see Roger, she still frowned. She didn't need a rescuer; she could handle her own problems.

"We were, but I realized The Wing Stop is closed on Sundays, and I thought I'd just stop by and wait. Then I saw Nathan here and—well, it seemed okay. Is it? Okay?" He looked confused.

Nathan patted his shoulder from behind. "Not really. We were just getting started. Get lost, Freeman."

The only thing he could possibly start at the moment was his exit strategy. Caroline really didn't care for Nathan. Sure, his girlfriend—scratch that—ex-girlfriend had been a bitch, but he wasn't exactly a pot of gold either. He was as slimy and greasy as that jungle-gym tube from the night before. She peeked at Roger, noting the uncertainty behind those brown eyes. He was unsure whether to stay or go—whether he'd interrupted something personal or business-focused. She clicked the flash off and dropped the camera to her side, giving him a laser-beam smile. "You know, I think I twisted something when I fell. Mind if we take a rain check, Nathan? Call this number and we can set up another time."

She flashed another business card his way, thankful she'd set up an answering service.

Nathan blinked and glanced from her to Roger then back. "Seriously?"

She nodded, her gaze focused on Roger. "Seriously."

Without warning, Roger leaned in and kissed her. Not one of the quick "hello" type pecks either—it was a long, deep, tonsil-lashing kiss that made her completely forget their audience.

"Okay then." Nathan's voice brought them both back to reality, and Roger stepped back. She could have sharpened a knife on the daggers Nathan shot at Roger before striding away. Roger watched him leave, then turned toward her and dimpled up. "Looks like I might be ousted from the house soon. Good thing I'm a senior."

"You know, I can handle his type."

"I'm sure you can, Caroline, but I'm not so sure I want you to. He's…slick."

She tapped a finger to his nose and whispered. "I vaguely remember you being *very* slick last night. And you shouldn't talk about one of your fraternity brothers that way."

His dimples didn't show. "I don't mean that kind of—"

Was he seriously about to give her a lecture on how to handle guys? She wasn't ten. "Speaking of slick, it took almost an entire bottle of shampoo to get that stuff out of my hair. Please tell me your kitchen doesn't cook with that stuff. Imagine what it'd do to your insides. Wherever we go to eat, I think I'm done with fried foods. How about salad?"

He lifted a brow.

"Okay, no salad. How about barbecue?"

"Sounds perfect. Maybe afterward we could throw Nathan on the pit, too." He hoisted the camera bag over a shoulder and grabbed her hand.

Two weeks later, Caroline rose from her seat in World Journalism class with a weight in her stomach. Two more weeks and they'd be off for the holidays. Winter break. One more semester closer to graduation.

"Ms. Sanders, may I have a moment?" Mr. Dennis, her instructor, called as she approached the door.

She turned. "Sure, what's up? I know I didn't do as well as hoped on the final, but—"

He held up a palm to silence her. "It's not that. I wanted you to take a look at this." He passed her a paper. "They're going to post it next week, but I thought of you when I read it. You mentioned wanting to do a traveling internship, right?"

Caroline read through the notice, which described a new website that advertised available internships abroad. She nodded. "Wow, thanks so much for thinking of me. What an opportunity."

"Yes, it is. I hope you find something and submit quickly—usually the first ones get a little more consideration."

The words sunk in further. He'd essentially just given her first dibs on any internship available. *Holy crap.*

"Yes, sir. Absolutely. I'll start looking tonight."

He frowned and shot one last instruction before he rushed to his office. "Whatever you choose…do a good job."

She hoped it would be good enough.

As she spotted Roger waving from outside the door, a small stone of uncertainty developed within her. She'd always planned on leaving, following her father's trail, but was that the right thing for her? Roger's welcoming dimples gave her confusing feelings about her future plans.

The fact that he'd waited for her made her feel safe. She wasn't sure how they'd evolved into—something. They just had. With no planning and zero effort, Roger had fallen into her life along with his clumsy dog. They'd simply showed up again on her step—over and over. First, he had come to replace the broken planter, then to fix her chair. After that, to get advice on a new camera. Another time to show her pictures from the party—she cringed at the way her damp clothing had revealed her boyish shape.

Each time they talked for hours while Conan lounged against their legs or rolled over to offer his massive chest for a massage. After a few days, she suggested they walk him around the campus and test his training. The dog flirted with every passerby, and he became so popular that on their fourth walk, one student even threw him a rawhide.

Roger wasn't really a boyfriend, but he was more than just a friend. They had begun "semidating" despite their pending graduation in the spring—only six months away. The realization brought Caroline an intense, tight panic. She didn't need this, not now—and the last thing she was ready for was a man who expected things of her. Someone who could trip her up while she planned her future. Her career. Her dream of becoming a journalist. She glanced at the paper in her shaking hand. The perfect opportunity—right within reach—and her instructor had thought her worthy enough to get a first shot.

She blinked. Being with Roger was easy, comfortable, and she craved him like she craved Reese's Peanut Butter Cups. She didn't need him in her life—he was a distraction—but God help her, she *wanted* him.

"Everything okay?" he asked when she joined him outside the classroom.

"Perfect." She slid the paper inside her backpack and tossed it over a shoulder as they headed for his car.

Chapter Six

After the first TKE frat party, Caroline was apprehensive about going with Roger to another, but he'd insisted. Still, she made a point of knowing the theme before agreeing to be his date. She surveyed her outfit and leaned toward the bathroom mirror to apply lip gloss and glitter. After all, Tinker Bell was covered in sparkle, right? A holiday sparkle-costume party sounded a lot less hazardous than the slippery ball-and-chain event. What could possibly go wrong with sparkle and glitter?

Her cell vibrated on the counter, and she snatched the device before it slipped to the floor.

Her mother's voice on the other side had a fatigued whine. "Hey, sweetie, what are you up to?"

Caroline grinned. "At the moment, I'm plastering myself in face glitter and fake eyelashes."

A giggle came through the earpiece. "Well, that's nice, though I never figured you for the fake-anything look."

Caroline shifted the phone to her shoulder and slipped into her black boots. While she'd doused herself in glitter and her sequined shirt reflected like a disco ball, she wasn't donning a skirt. She didn't feel like baring her legs in the cold. "I'm going to a frat party—as Tinker Bell. Can you believe that? A friend of mine asked me to come, and he should be here soon. Everything okay there?"

A couple seconds of silence made her wonder if she'd lost the connection. "Yeah, yeah, I just wanted to make sure you're planning to come home for winter break."

Caroline flicked off the light and strode toward the closet to retrieve a jacket. "Of course I am. What else would I do? We have finals next week, and I'll leave after my last test. I'll let you know then. Gotta go, Mom, my friend's here."

She clicked the phone just as Roger rapped on the door. She felt guilty for not divulging more about their friendship, but she wasn't quite ready to expose him to her world. His world was so much bigger and bolder; hers was quiet and simple. And perhaps a tad boring. She hated hanging up on her mother, too, but time was limited. Besides, they'd talk for hours once she made it home for break—it could wait until then.

Caroline whisked the door opened and thrust her tongue into her cheek to stifle a laugh. She cast her gaze up and down Roger's costume. "Well, that's certainly full of sparkle."

Roger held out his arms and did a very Motown-ish twirl in a deep-plum sequined suit. Or was it a tuxedo? "Isn't it awesome? I found it at a thrift shop."

She crossed her arms over her chest. "I'm getting visions of matadors, Michael Jackson, and—"

He whisked his hand from his back and held out a royal-blue felt hat, then pointed at his toes. "I'm a rhinestone cowboy. See. Check out this hat." With a flick of his wrist, he rolled the hat atop his brown waves and lifted his lips into a slow, devious grin.

Caroline felt the increasingly familiar kick of warmth and released a giggle. "Ha. Tinker Bell and Tinseltown. Aren't we a pair?"

Roger crooked his arm for her and bowed. "You ready, Tink?"

She squinted up at the light over the front door. Between their sequined bodies and the glow above, a kaleidoscope of color danced over her steps. Slipping a hand into his arm, she bounded down and headed to the party.

The evening was surreal—like waking up in the middle of *Ever After*. Caroline imagined that those wings on Drew Barrymore's costume would have made an awesome addition to her Tinker Bell get-up.

Once the slow music started and Roger pulled her tight, she realized wings would have severely hampered her ability to get close to him. Forget the wings. Wings are highly overrated.

"You look blissful—like you just ate an entire bag of potato chips." As Roger's big browns focused on her face, she noted there was a swipe of glitter on his chin. Had that come from her? And how had he discovered her fetish for salty chips?

"This is better. So much better. All these lights and people dressed up like a ball. It's perfect." She waved at their surroundings.

"You're perfect."

Was he teasing? His eyes held no mirth. She knew she wasn't even close to perfect, but it was nice to hear.

"Yeah, right."

She peeked over his shoulder and noted Nathan approaching. "Creep alert, two o'clock."

Roger glanced at his fraternity brother. "Hey, give him a break. You can't fault the guy for trying to date perfection. I'm just glad I found you first."

Caroline wasn't sure he'd technically *found* her, but she registered the compliment. "I don't think you actually found me so much as kidnapped me."

"Details are irrelevant." Roger wrapped an arm over her shoulder and drew her close. He kissed her hair. "Besides, you *are* with the hottest cowboy here, and I've been told girls love guys in boots and cowboy hats."

She cocked a brow. "I don't think that includes sequined suits that likely belonged to a Prince wannabe."

"I could always take it off," he whispered in her hair.

Whoa. The vision that crossed her mind made her blood pressure hitch. "I'm not sure that's a good idea here."

"Who said anything about here?" He grinned.

Music blared from a speaker system. "I'm not sleeping with you, Roger."

"Ahem." Nathan stood behind Roger in a bedazzled T-shirt, which was the extent of his costume.

"Hi, Nathan. Nice shirt." Caroline kept her voice chipper as Roger's arm clenched a bit on her shoulder. "I love the theme of this party. I'd much rather wash glitter from my hair than goo—though the oily stuff was kind of fun." She shot a sideways glance at Roger. Nathan would get the wrong idea from her innuendo, but who cared?

"Thanks. This was my idea. The entertainment crew split up the party themes and drew numbers at the beginning of the year to decide who planned which event. I pulled this one."

"Nice," Roger answered.

Nathan shrugged. "Hey, we needed to do something classy before everyone disappeared for the holidays. Plus we have to celebrate the end of finals. Don't forget to get a picture taken in the photo booth over there. It won't be as professional as Caroline's, but you need something to remember." Nathan introduced them to a short blonde with a halo of curls and a silver glittered ring atop her head to match. Caroline and Roger smiled and waved then hooked arms and wandered away.

Green Day blared over the speaker system, and Roger pulled Caroline toward the music. Caroline loved their tunes and happily joined the mass of dancers on the floor, dripping glitter along the way.

An hour later, they were covered in sweat and sparkle. Roger grabbed a few beers from an open ice pit. "It's suffocating. Let's cool off outside," he said. With her hair in damp ringlets, she had no problem following him.

Outside, Roger walked her around the grounds of their fraternity compound. It was aesthetically pleasing in a fancy way, even if the interior was filled with stolen street signs, bar lights, and posters of half-naked women. She'd glanced in a few bedrooms as she sought out the bathroom earlier.

"Caroline, about that sleeping-together thing." They were going to have that discussion now? Seriously?

"I said I'm not sleeping with you."

He grinned. "Technically, you already have. I've been at your place at least three or four times a week."

She rolled her eyes. "That doesn't count." She didn't dare admit she'd thought about giving him a little drawer space to stash a change of clothes.

Roger's eyes glinted in the flicker of the strings of white light that hung from the fences outside. "Hey, it counts for me. So, what are you doing over the holiday break? Are you heading home or staying?"

Glad for a change of focus, Caroline took a sip of her beer. "I'm going home."

He hesitated for a second, and she watched his Adam's apple lunge as he searched for the right words. "I was hoping I could talk you into spending a couple of days at my house."

"Here?"

He shrugged. "Not exactly. My family always has a big family thing. It's not a big deal, but you'd probably enjoy yourself—no pressure or anything. I just think they'd, I don't know, maybe like you?"

Oh God, he wanted her to meet his family? Her face flushed, and the sweat on her forehead instantly dried. That sounded serious.

"I can't. It's just my mother and me. My dad's gone."

"Oh, I'm sorry. We never really talked about that."

"No, he's not *dead*. He's just…I don't know. Last I heard, he was in France on an assignment. He's a journalist. I have seen him all of six times since I was about sixteen."

"So they're split up?"

She sighed. "Who knows. We're pretty screwed up. She doesn't talk about it, and I don't ask. Pretty weird, huh?"

Their eyes met for a second, and she thought she saw a little pity buried in the depths of his. She didn't want pity. He watched her over the rim of his Solo cup as he slugged back the rest of his beer. "Maybe she could come, too?"

She shook her head in disbelief. "Uh-uh. No way. We hardly know each other, and you're asking me to bring my family to your house? That's—crazy. Besides, what's the point? She doesn't need to know you. I'll be gone in a few months. I don't want her getting attached."

I don't even want ME getting attached.

Chapter Seven

Roger loved being home for holidays. It was a little claustrophobic being surrounded by his sisters, but it was also the only time when they all were converged at the house together. He missed that part of his childhood.

He stood in the kitchen sipping iced tea as his mother, Ruth, and youngest sister, Rebecca, chopped vegetables and stirred bowls of unknown goo dubbed—the latest "dip" recipe he was sure to enjoy. All of them were on diets each time he saw them, so veggies were a staple. For them, not him. He could care less about the slight beer belly he'd taken on since freshman year. He patted it affectionately and took another sip of tea. "Where's Dad?"

His mother's eyes were swollen and red. She must have been up late working on the food for the day. She shot her gaze at the ceiling. "Work, of course. They're swamped, and he's there almost every night. If he's not there, he's on the phone with one client or another. If you ask me, they need to hire some help."

Roger frowned. His father had never missed these celebrations before—he loved having everyone together. *Odd.*

The door banged open then shut as footsteps thundered up from the basement garage. He must be home.

"Hello!" Definitely not Dad's voice. There was no mistaking his oldest sibling's high-pitched squeal for their father's. She rounded the corner and flung herself against Roger's chest, sloshing tea down his chin.

"Rhianna, chill. You spilled my drink." He wiped the splatter from his shirt, tossed the tea glass in the sink, and wrapped her in a bear hug. "How's that new job going?" Last he'd heard, she was working for a state horticulture agency on a sustainable living project. She always loved a cause—any cause really—and flitted from one to the next.

Rhianna waved a hand. "It's a job. Did Emma show this time?"

Their middle sister hadn't attended many of the family events the past couple of years. She'd had a blow-out with their Dad from what Roger heard. She avoided the subject when he called. "Nope. Mom said she's on a ski trip with a group."

"When did she learn how to ski?"

Roger laughed, then made his way into the den and plopped onto his dad's chair, stretching his legs over the worn ottoman. There was something comforting about the spot his father had staked claim to—it was worn with age, yet no one dared move or replace anything. Hearing the sound of a motor, he sat up to see his father's car pull into the crowded drive. About time the old man showed.

Roger noted the shadow of his father still behind the wheel. Was he talking on his cell?

Roger waved. His father returned the gesture and extricated himself from the car as he stuffed his phone into a pocket. The minute Eric Freeman stepped inside, Roger felt the chill. His mother stayed in the kitchen while his father made the round of hugs with Roger and his sisters.

Something wasn't right. Both his father and mother wore red-rimmed eyes like hay-fever sufferers. Hers seemed pooled with near-tears. His were just plain red. When they'd finished their meal and caught up on everyone's lives, his mom picked up dishes and disappeared to the kitchen. The sisters followed. Roger stared at his father. "Dad, what's going on?"

Mason Eric Freeman, known as Eric by his friends and family, steepled his fingers over his empty plate, his elbows planted firmly on the table. "Nothing. Everything's fine. Everything's *going* to be fine. Don't worry. We'll talk about it later—after everyone settles down."

Settles down? What the hell was that supposed to mean?

Eric's cell chimed in his pocket and he excused himself to take the call, striding toward the bathroom. He returned forty-five minutes later while they were all lounging in the den. "We have something to tell you," Eric said. He motioned for Ruth to stand and join him, but she stayed in her seat.

Outside, Conan barked for attention. A reminder that Roger had left him tied to the steps far too long.

"What's up?" Rebecca asked. Her voice was cheerful, yet Roger registered the dread in her eyes. Whatever they were about to say, she knew more than the rest. Roger narrowed his eyes at her, and she blinked. Was she about to cry?

Eric frowned at his wife. "Are you gonna help me out here? Or do I have to do this myself?"

She shrugged. "Seems to me like you haven't been doing *anything* by yourself in quite some time. Nor have you done it with—"

Eric held up a hand. "Stop. Look, guys. I know this is bad timing, but we're hardly ever together anymore. It seemed better to tell everyone in person rather than trying to track each of you down separately. Your mother and I have agreed—to take some time off."

Roger sucked in his breath as if punched in the gut. Any time someone leads with the words "bad timing" whatever follows can't be good.

Rhianna jumped up to hug her mother. "A vacation! That's awesome. Where are you going?"

"Not that kind of time off, idiot," Roger snapped.

Ruth patted Rhianna's arm and wrestled free. Her jaw was taut with forced composure. "No, honey. Your dad's moving out for a while. He needs to—hell, I don't know what he needs." She rushed out. A moment later, the bedroom door closed.

Roger was torn between chasing after his mother and punching his dad in the face. Fortunately, Rhianna ran toward the closed door, leaving them sitting in silence. A glance at his youngest sister confirmed tears streaming down her cheeks. She sat silently staring at her hands. With clenched fists, Roger leveled his gaze on his father. "Dad?"

Eric hung his head as if the word stung. "I just can't do it anymore. I'm sorry. Roger, you need to grow up—and fast. It's time you started helping out and paying your share. Your mother's going to need you."

"Are you *crazy*? Or maybe sick or something? You're our *dad* for Christ's sake…the guy who took me fishing and camping. Hell, you *molded* me. If this is about Mom, maybe it's just an empty-nester thing. We're almost all gone now—that can't be easy, but it's no reason to cut and run. You two should celebrate. You should be going somewhere *together*. Getting to know each other again…"

Without lifting his eyes, Eric shook his head. "I can't do it, son. I've tried. It's just not working."

"*What* can't you do? Pay the bills? I can get a part-time job and pay for school if that's the issue. I only need one more semester to finish. I—"

Roger's father turned his back on the room—too cowardly to face them. "The money isn't the issue. I've lived all my life working to make everyone else happy, helping all of you find your way. Not once in all that time have I ever had a chance to find my own. I have to do this—for me. I met someone, Roger, someone who understands me and tries to make *me* happy. She's fantastic, and I finally feel like I'm discovering who I am—or at least like I've found a path. We work together. I'm leaving my job, and soon we're going off on our own. We can't afford to get off to a bad start. Just know that I love you very much."

Eric Freeman left the room without looking any of his children in the eye. This was for him? Was there nothing about his family that made him happy? It was all too much a burden, all those years together? Jesus, was he for real?

What a fricking piece of work.

Chapter Eight

Caroline's time with her mother was too brief, but she was glad to return to school and have some privacy. Her mother was a hoverer, and while it was nice to be pampered, it got old in a matter of hours. Refreshed and reenergized, Caroline delved into her new and final semester with vigor. At night she researched and applied to potential internships—and debated texting Roger. Surely a simple "what's up" would be okay? But she refrained.

Caroline stared at the blank screen of her cell phone. Roger had left for the holidays without a word. Now four weeks had passed without a call. Jesus, he could at least let her know he was okay, right? Just because she had refused to meet his family didn't mean they couldn't hang out.

She had intended to just leave Roger alone after he'd asked her—*and her mother*—to his family celebration. She had freaked and shut it down. What was the point when they'd both graduate in May and go their separate ways? They hadn't known each other long enough to disrupt their lives for—whatever they had.

Caroline grabbed a pile of mail from her mailbox and thumbed through. The *New York Times*. Holy cow, was this a response to her internship application? Could she be so lucky? She ripped the envelope open and surveyed the letter. She'd been accepted for one of five traveling news internships, each in a different territory, all of which were a plane flight away. "I got it! Oh my God, I got it!"

She jumped up and down and pumped her fist in the air. Her plan was falling into place. She started to grab her phone to call Roger. But after rereading the words, she hesitated. It was an *unpaid* internship, with no guarantee of future employment. Still, it was *something*.

She stuffed the acceptance letter in her camera bag—a nice little reminder of the bright career ahead. She'd seen her father's journalistic work, and as good as it looked, she knew she could do better—or at least equally well. But things with Roger were somehow unfinished. They'd been hot and heavy before the break, but only in a temporary, college-fling way. Then she blew it.

Why had he ruined everything by asking her to go home with him? Ugh. The thought of meeting his family brought chills to her soul. It wasn't that she hadn't wanted to meet them; she just wasn't ready. There was something *permanent* about doing so—which seemed irresponsible considering her plans to be gone by summer.

It had been awkward. In the end, Roger just held her gaze for five long seconds. She knew for how long because she'd counted in her head while waiting for him to say something. He hadn't said a word—just shrugged, shoved his hands in his pockets, and strode off without a care. Her pride hadn't allowed her to ask if he would call while he was gone—or if she'd see him when he returned. She assumed he would.

Bad assumption.

Her phone chimed to remind her of a pending photo session at a fiftieth-anniversary party off-campus. Not only were they married a hell of a long time, but the couple had both served in the military and were decorated vets. *This should be fun.* A day full of war stories and travel memories. It was sure to make the average two-hour gig stretch into four or five hours.

Caroline hoped not—she wanted to go to the beach before dark. She'd even put her swimsuit on under the skirt and T-shirt she'd donned for the party. The strings of her bikini top were tucked under the neck—no one would notice. She had an hour to get to the party and set up—fifteen minutes was all that she required. She turned the camera on for one last check. Batteries charged. Extra batteries packed. Memory chips in outside pocket. She flipped the button to review the current memory chip and see if she needed to swap it out. Yep, it was full. She popped it out and inserted a spare then checked again.

Oh, crap.

Pictures of Roger's frat brother, Nathan, stared her in the face from their short moments on campus. She'd never rescheduled his photo session. She scrolled through the snapshots. Wow, not bad considering the deception she'd used to get them. He looked… nice. She grinned, acknowledging her talent with a camera. Nathan was definitely not nice—but she'd taken some great pictures. She should call him and offer to show them. She popped out the card slid and empty one into place.

With the camera stowed in her car, she decided to end her vow of silence with Roger. After all, she knew what it was like to just stop talking, and it wasn't a good feeling. Her dad had all but abandoned them in search of his big story, and she wouldn't do the same to people she cared about. She wouldn't let it happen again, and she wouldn't let their friendship drift off into the unknown. It was too hurtful.

Five minutes later, she turned into Roger's driveway and honked. Yeah, it was annoying and lame, but so was his apathy. Conan's barking thundered through the walls followed by Roger's voice as he shushed the dog. Caroline stepped from the car and approached the door. Halfway there, the screen screeched open.

"Caroline…Hi. What are you doing?" His face was shadowed in days of beard growth. His shoulders sagged. Roger appeared… ill. He looked like hell warmed over.

Her heart twisted. She'd intended to be mad—confrontational, even. But his hair shagged around his cheekbones and dipped into the crevices of the missing dimples. Several days of growth on his chin made him look like he'd been on a four-week hunting trip instead of a family holiday celebration.

Something had happened. His haggard face and soft brown eyes gave her the feeling that an interrogation wouldn't be appropriate. Perhaps he needed warmth or acceptance instead. She softened her voice. "I was wondering the same thing about you. Are you sick?"

His smile was a façade. "No, I'm good. It's just—"

Caroline closed the gap between them and stood inches from his face. The shadows of the beard weren't the only rough edges on Roger; his eyes were clouded and grim. "Look," she said, "I wanted to explain. I, um, panicked when you asked me to go with you. I wasn't ready for a big family thing."

Roger rubbed the back of his neck with his fingers. "Don't worry about it. In fact, things would have been more awkward with you there. My parents split up."

Holy crap. No wonder he'd been silent for days. "Oh, my God. I'm so sorry—are you okay?" She placed her fingers on his forearm, not sure if he'd jerk away.

"Yep. It's good. I'm good. All is…good. He just decided out of the blue that he needed to 'find his way.' Can you believe that shit? What the hell does that mean? He's a grown man. If he doesn't know who the hell he is or what his fricking way is, it's a little late now. What the hell has he been doing all this time?"

Caroline focused on his face, waiting for him to meet her gaze. "I don't know what to say. I, uh, I'm sorry."

He studied her for a minute; she felt his eyes drop to her lips then lift to meet hers. "It's not your fault."

"It's not yours either."

Roger said nothing.

Caroline swallowed against a wad of cotton-like dryness in her mouth. What the hell do you say to comfort someone in such a situation? She hadn't a clue. Her father had been out of the picture for a while, and it still stung. Maybe nothing? Perhaps he needed to get away from the drama? She gulped. "I have a gig this afternoon, but I planned to head to the beach after and take some pictures for a project. I know it's probably not all that exciting but…you wanna come along?"

"What kind of gig?"

Her stomach sank—of all things, did it have to be an anniversary party? "Fiftieth anniversary for a couple of veterans. You don't have to come along—I probably shouldn't have asked." What a dumb suggestion.

"No, I'll go. The beach sounds great. I'm…not sure about the other thing, but hey, you probably need someone to carry your gear, right?" He offered a genuine smile, and Caroline's heart squeezed again—lord, she'd missed his dimples.

"If I needed a pack mule, I could always ask your buddy, Nathan," she teased.

He snickered. "Go for it—I dare you."

She lifted a brow, but the playful gesture was lost on Roger as he turned to lock his door. In fact, he remained fairly quiet until the party ended and they arrived at the beach. She spread the blanket she'd packed, set her camera gear down, and pulled off her shirt to reveal her bikini top.

Roger tsked. "No more polka dots?"

"This is my swimsuit, not my underwear."

"I figured as much. I like the look. So, when you said veteran's anniversary earlier, I wasn't expecting a wedding anniversary."

A ting of guilt thumped Caroline in the head. She had been slightly evasive, but it wasn't intended to be hurtful. "Under the circumstances, I was afraid you'd say no. Was it uncomfortable? I saw you dancing with the bride's nieces and nephews, so I assumed you were okay."

"Not uncomfortable at all. In fact, it was perfect. Good to see that some people really *can* make it work despite the statistics."

Caroline pulled her camera from its compartment and turned to snap a trio of seagulls that swooped low seeking crumbs. She laughed when they dove closer. "I'm starting to think I smell like fish."

Roger squinted into the bright sky. "They're attracted to the reflection off your camera. Better watch out: this could get ugly."

A gull swooped in and grabbed a few strands of her hair, yanking as it pulled away. "Holy crap! They want to eat me. Do I look like breadcrumbs or something? They must be desperate."

Roger broke into full smile. "I'd say you look more like candy. They're not desperate; they're just craving something sweet."

Oh, that was nice. Caroline flapped her arms over her head and beaned one of the birds with her camera. It screeched, and the tiny flock scattered. Whew, bird-pecking crisis averted.

Roger dropped down onto the blanket. He raised a knee and propped his arm across it. "That was a pretty cool ceremony earlier. Sad and inspiring at the same time. Sad because I know I'll never be one of those people, but inspiring because they were heroes in more ways than we can count. They served our country. They obviously were good parents if you judge the number of children and grandchildren running around. They looked genuinely happy, too—which surprised me."

Caroline lowered to her knees beside him and placed the camera on the blanket. "It's so rare to see people at their age who still like each other and want to be together. Or at least it seems rare."

He nodded. "Makes me want to be them."

"Old and feeble with no memory?"

Roger's hair flapped in the wind as he shook his head. "Since my dad decided to…do his thing, I've thought a lot about life and family. I have this theory."

Her attempt to lighten the mood had failed miserably. She leaned back onto her elbows and sprawled her feet in front of her. "Okay, let's hear it."

"I think people have three basic needs in life, no matter their age. Without those three fulfilled, they can't survive. Or at least not happily. The first one is obviously sustenance: food and water. The second is shelter."

Caroline blinked and turned to watch waves crash to shore nearby. "Of course."

"I guess, but that could mean a lot of things. It could be a house or a tent, a mansion, or a cabin in the woods. That's where all our nonessential wants come into play. None of it would matter if the third need were perfect. That's the most important one."

The conversation had officially gotten seriously deep. Caroline felt a chill roll over her shoulders. She debated pulling her shirt on, but she clutched her knees instead and waited for him to finish. The clouds were fading to pink around the edges, a reminder she wanted to take a few more pictures before dark. Still he needed to say whatever was on his mind.

"The third need—which most people neglect but in reality is probably the biggest—is a purpose. People have to feel like they have a passion, a reason for being here and tromping to work every day. A reason for paying the bills and putting up with that nagging boss or whiny coworker. That's what we're all seeking."

Caroline leveled her gaze on him. He was serious. "You know, I totally agree. I have always thought that's what was missing. I've wanted to be a journalist since I was twelve, and I can't wait until I graduate and can get out there and start working. For some reason, it feels like walking away from a tied game in the ninth inning. You don't want to leave it undecided. My dad's been gone for—a while— on assignment. I haven't seen him in forever. He's a journalist, too."

"You told me that already."

"I know, but you see, that's just it: it's in my blood. I know that's what I'm meant to be."

"You do? I envy you then. I don't have a clue what I want. I just said that because I've been trying to understand how someone could leave a wife and four kids after twenty-plus years. I wonder if I ever will. I always thought that was the utopia we all yearned for—you know, a good job, a family, a nice place to live, enough money to enjoy life."

Caroline studied Roger's face. She understood—she'd tried to rationalize her own father's absence for years. It hadn't worked. Roger's brown eyes darkened with emotion, the lines of his smile barely a ripple. The wind from the sea washed over him, warm and loving, tousling his hair and clothes. He stared off at the waves, giving her a chance to drink in the smell of his Polo cologne and the way his eyes creased at the corners.

"Well, I'd better get those pictures done. I need them for my project, and it's due in a week," she said.

"Plenty of time. I usually wait 'til the night before." He teased.

"It's a major grade. I have to create a news article complete with photos that evoke emotion. We'll be graded on the intensity of both the picture and the associated news article."

Roger squinted again. "What are planning? You're obviously doing a beach theme, so what's the focus?"

Caroline pointed at the weathered remains of a sea wall with a crumbled pier jutting from the rough rock. "We're supposed to write about something that impacts our city or campus. I think most people are doing something about student activities on campus, so I wanted to be different. I thought I'd showcase various off-campus activities instead. That abandoned pier, for example."

"How does that dilapidated hunk of wood relate to our alma mater?" He looked skeptical.

"While perusing the internship boards looking for postgrad work, I came across a civil group whose mission is to 'restore and revive' that pier. Apparently a small group of brown pelicans use it as their home post. They're protected in this area, but their pier was demolished in the last hurricane. It looked like it could be a different and interesting human-interest story."

"Caroline, I don't really see how a group of dislocated pelicans can evoke the level of emotion your instructor intended. Are you sure you want to risk a major grade on this?"

"It's an environmental issue, an animal rights issue, and a story of rebuilding after disaster. How is that a risk?"

What the heck had he expected? Another sob story about how hard students work? Or how little funding the university has for their programs? One of her classmates had divulged his project was focused on better security for students. A very important theme, yes. Interesting, too, but predictable. At least hers was original. Roger watched the waves roll onto the beach while Caroline snapped a memory card into the camera, changed the lens, and strode toward the pier. She half-expected him to follow. Instead he entwined his fingers behind his head and lay backward onto the blanket.

When Caroline returned, Roger had kicked off his shoes and removed his shirt. It was hard not to focus on the tiny hairs that feathered down the center of his chest and teased at the top of his shorts. They were soft and brown and begging to be touched. She dropped on the blanket and pulled open her camera bag to return her equipment.

Roger popped an eye open. "Good, you're back. Let's take a dip in the water."

"Now? It's going to be dark soon."

"Not for at least another forty-five minutes. You have your suit on. Come with me." He rose to his feet and beckoned for her to follow him to the water's edge.

"You're not wearing trunks. You're gonna swim in your shorts?"

He gave her a sly grin. "You sound like you want me to swim out of them. That's good with me." He reached for the zipper.

Caroline held out a hand. "No! I hadn't planned on bailing your naked ass out of jail today."

Roger laughed. She was relieved to see the dimples. "Who's gonna arrest me, Caro? There's not a soul on the beach except us. Don't worry, I was kidding. These shorts'll work fine. I'm going in." He turned and did exactly as he promised. In a few short jogs,

Roger was up to his knees in sea froth. He lowered to his waist and allowed the sea swells to crest over his head.

Perspiration beaded on Caroline's forehead, daring her to join him in the water. No further encouragement needed. She unzipped and dropped her skirt, stepped out of the pile of fabric, and then kicked through the sand to the water's edge. Roger was already shoulder-deep, and the silver glare of rippled waves reflected against his skin in a shiny flutter. She ignored the urge to run back and retrieve her camera for a few quick shots.

It took about a minute to work through the water to his side. Once there, the undertow shoved her against him with one hard toss. "Wow, the pull is strong."

"I get that a lot. Don't fight it; I can't help being irresistible."

Caroline waved her arms under the surface to stay afloat. "I think I can manage to control myself."

The water tossed her into him again, and Roger quirked a brow. "You're doing a great job."

She put a hand on his chest and pushed off, but before she'd gained distance he grabbed her wrist and pulled her back. Roger wrapped his arms around her waist. Droplets hung from his lashes, turning them into tiny starbursts. "I should have called you. My mind's been a little messed up about my parents. Can you forgive me?"

Forgiving him was easy, but the discomfort she'd felt the past couple of weeks confused her. Could he forgive *her* for dissing his request to meet his family? Or could she forgive herself for getting this involved? "What are we doing, Roger?"

With one palm gripping her back to hold them together, he rubbed the saltwater from his eyes. "Haven't you ever wanted to take a sunset swim? Put your arms around my neck and float. I've got you."

She followed the orders but frowned. "I wasn't talking about swimming. I meant…this. Us. I'm graduating at the end of this semester, and I just received my acceptance letter for an internship with the Times. It'll involve traveling overseas. It might lead to a real journalism job in New York."

He sobered. "You'll leave."

It wasn't the words that bothered her; it was more the way he'd said them and his gloomy expression. It wasn't as if she planned to follow his father's example—to run away from something big and long term. How could he throw so much accusation into two tiny words? They hadn't even been together that long—hell, *were* they together? He'd spent a lot of time at her place up until he went home. Then nothing. She'd heard nothing from him. Not one word.

Something swished gently against Caroline's butt cheek. "Hey, stop that."

"What?"

"Stop trying to grab my ass."

"How am I gonna do that when I'm holding you up with both hands?"

Oh, good point. She noted his fingers wrapped around her lower waist. Unless he'd grown another appendage, something else had—

"Holy crap, something just swam against me." She kicked the water, churning it into a boil. If his hands were occupied, that had to be a fish—a fairly big fish.

A fin popped up nearby. Caroline screamed.

Chapter Nine

Roger sucked in a deep breath and stumbled backward as Caroline dug her foot into his groin and wrapped her arms around his head. As she flung a leg over his shoulder, trying to crawl up his body, he widened his stance to hold her weight. He gulped in water and tried to speak, but his mouth was smashed against her belly button. Normally that would be awesome, but she would drown both of them if she kept flailing.

He'd seen the fin—the *dolphin* fin. He coughed and tried again to voice his thoughts. "Caroline, calm *down*."

"Where'd it go? I can't see it! He's under the water. Oh, my God! Swim, Roger, swim!" She let go and shoved a foot into his shoulder, then started wildly kicking her legs as she swam toward the beach. If it had been a real shark, they would've been doomed. In the distance, he saw a dark sheen rise on the surface and roll back under the water.

"It's gone, Caroline. You scared it away." She was splashing like a drowning horse, so she heard nothing. Laughter bubbled inside him for the first time in weeks. Several feet away, she darted a glance back then stood thigh-deep and motioned frantically for him to follow. At least she showed a small amount of concern for his safety. He swam after her. Once the water became shallow enough to stand, he rose and shook his hair—then let the laughter roll, hard and loud. He laughed until his stomach pinched his sides, then clutched his ribcage and laughed some more.

Caroline slammed her hands onto her hips. "What is so fricking funny?"

Tears stung his eyes and he sucked in a huge breath to gain composure. "It was a dolphin, Caroline. A harmless Bambi of the water. It wasn't going to hurt us. It was probably just curious."

"Hey, when something big, dark, and slimy rubs against you under the waves, you don't stop to ask what species it might be or if it's going to eat you. You assume it's the big bad wolf and you get the hell out. Besides, how do you know dolphins are harmless? Just because they say that on television doesn't mean they're safe. They might not have ten thousand massive teeth like sharks, but they still have *some*."

She had a point, but he was still trying to compose himself. He sucked in another breath. "Holy wave-runner, that was funny."

"Stop laughing."

He ran a hand over his mouth and jammed it inward as if attempting to stifle his bellows. "I'm trying. I'm trying. You realize I would have been shark bait if it were really dangerous? You deserted me!"

"I did not."

"No, you *climbed* me like a buoy."

"Well, you *were* the tallest thing out there and sturdy as a rock. I wasn't trying to sacrifice you or anything. You just seemed…safe. Safer than the water."

"Thanks. I think." Roger's feet felt like lead. He pushed out of the water and followed Caroline to the blanket. A memory flooded through his head. "When I was a kid, we visited my grandparents in south Texas. There was a rainstorm, and their front yard flooded nearly to their door. We watched out the window and wondered if we should evacuate. After a while, there were little reddish-brown things floating across the water. I thought they were piles of sticks and leaves, but they moved like molten lava. You know what they were?"

She pulled a towel out of her bag and dried off before sprawling atop the blanket. She closed her eyes. "No idea."

"They were piles of ants. You know what they were doing? Crawling atop the dead bodies of other ants to float above the water. They sacrificed themselves to save others and their queen. You crawling up me like a ladder made me think of it."

She opened her eyes and leveled her gaze on him. "I panicked, but I wasn't planning to sacrifice you. You know that, right?" She rolled onto her stomach.

"It's okay. I don't mind being a worker ant." *Especially when half-naked women need saving.* He dropped beside her and dragged the towel over his legs and torso. Her eyes remained closed, and after a few minutes, he noted her quiet, rhythmic breathing. Was she asleep? He crouched closer and peered at her eyelids. Yep, she was out. How could she go from scared shitless to sound asleep in such a short time? Crazy. He shook his head.

The light shimmered across her skin. The wind pulled a corner of the blanket up and tickled it across her back. With closed eyes, she swatted as if it were a fly.

Roger stilled beside her and closed his eyes too. He couldn't sleep—too much adrenaline flowing. He opened an eye and glanced sideways. The sun danced across her skin—it was fascinating. She'd untied the tie of her top, which lay pooled beside her.

Roger slowly and quietly reached into her camera bag, inserted a new memory card, and snapped a couple shots of her. Had she heard the click? He lowered the lens and waited, half expecting an outburst. No movement. The wind blasted him. *The breeze is carrying the sound away from her.* How convenient. He snapped more then rose as quietly as possible and zoomed to get the last few from a distance. When he was done, he pulled the memory card and dropped it in his pocket, pleased with his efforts. The pictures weren't obscene, just strange…and stunningly fresh. He'd never seen sand sparkle like glass—or maybe he'd just never noticed before. It was almost festive.

Chapter Ten

They were graduating in less than three weeks, and for the life of him, Roger couldn't fathom his future. He hadn't avoided Caroline after the holidays. He'd simply accepted the inevitable.

That she planned to leave.

Like his father, she had to search out her place in life. He silently tsked—at least *she* wasn't waiting until she had children and a spouse of twenty-five years to make such a discovery. He stared at his ethics book, wishing the pages would reveal the answer to his own destiny. Why does an old man forsake his upbringing and values for a new relationship with a younger woman? What was he seeking that he hadn't already achieved? Obviously his father hadn't studied ethics.

The ethics exam was the next day, and he was already ready. Studying was a ruse to spend more time with Caroline. Her final project deadline fell just after his exam, and she was scrambling to perfect the words. Prose. Voice. Literary mumbo jumbo.

He toed off his shoes and sprawled on her couch while she bent over her laptop at the kitchen counter. From a distance, he had a good view of her concentration. The strength of a mountain resided in that tiny frame, along with the determination and confidence he lacked. She was crazy-focused. Confident in her goal, if not herself. He already possessed plenty of confidence; it just wasn't zeroed in on the future. He was completely comfortable with himself, but his choice of degree scared the hell out of him. He couldn't imagine what the future held. One thing was certain: his family needed support and stability. They would have a steep hill to climb over the next few months—or years—while his dad sorted out his issues.

Roger had fully intended to let Caroline go before she showed up at his doorstep and asked him to accompany her to the beach.

Was it the sunshine, the water, or seeing her enraptured face reposed on a blanket that made his feelings flip-flop? Maybe it was her assurance and bold determination to pursue her dreams. She knew where she was going and what she'd do to get there. People *follow* that kind of determination. Hell, he wanted to be a part.

"I've been thinking a lot about your trip to Europe for that internship." His voice croaked. Every ounce of moisture had left his parched throat as he weighed his words.

Caroline lifted her head and met his gaze with wide-eyed anticipation. "Me too. I Googled the countries best for the research and printed out some maps. I'm so excited."

It was impossible not to be infected by her excitement, but somewhere inside him a mounting fear half-stepped up a ladder of anxiety. He swallowed. "Is anyone going with you on this trip?"

Silence. The look on her face suggested she'd never even considered bringing company. It shocked him. Many women her age wouldn't even go to the bathroom alone, but she was so used to being on her own she'd planned to travel the world in solitude. He hated the idea. Caroline took a sip from a tea glass at her side. "What do you mean?"

"Is this a group trip you're involved with? A journalism club or something?"

She shook her head. "Real journalists don't exactly travel in groups like on a tour bus. I have to do this alone, to meld with the local culture and weed out a good story. That's what my dad did—does."

Roger narrowed his eyes, feeling the raging desire to scoop her into an enormous hug. "Caroline, you know you can't make him come back into your life simply by following his footsteps."

She slammed the glass to the counter. A splash of tea erupted and landed near her forearm. "That's not what I'm doing. Besides he's in my life—sort of. He sends things to my mother."

"Like what?"

"News clippings. Copies of research on the project he's working on. Little notes."

"That's enough for you?" He realized the words were combative and cold, but he wanted to know. Was she really okay with such a nonexistent parental relationship? Would he ever get to that point with his own father?

Caroline shut the lid to her laptop with a click and padded barefoot to the couch. She dropped beside him and stretched her legs across his. "No, but it's all I get."

Roger's heart squeezed. "So you chose the same profession and decided to trek around the world in search of him."

She jutted her chin out and lifted her head in defiance. "That's not what this is about. This is about doing what I'm meant to do. Fulfilling my purpose in life. My passion. Why are you trying to ruin it?"

God, he wished he knew what that meant. "Caro, gorgeous. I'm not trying to ruin anything; I'm just afraid for you. There's a lot of bad people in this world who would see a young, beautiful woman in a foreign country as an easy target. Easy prey."

Her eyes softened a smidge. "Journalists are protected under the Geneva Convention—we have safe passage."

She really believed in that crap? He stroked a finger over her kneecap. "According to the Geneva Convention, *anyone* who isn't part of a war is guaranteed safe passage. That means all civilians and travelers. But bad things still happen."

Caroline frowned. "What do you expect me to do then?"

He leveled his gaze and calculated the impact of his next words. Would she be open to the idea? He'd never considered it until recently, but his thoughts were consumed now. The thought of taking over his family financial burdens lingered like the taste of bitter lemons. It wasn't *his* responsibility, so why the hell had his dad given him this burden? His entire body ached with a longing to feel what Caroline felt as she anticipated her upcoming adventure. God, he wished for such enthusiasm. A chance to attack the world with vigor and leave the disappointment and ruined dreams behind to find new ones. "Take me with you."

He heard the faucet drip in the kitchen. Splat. Splat. Splat. Her eyes concentrated on his fingers as they circled the skin on her knee. Water pooled in her lower lids and spilled slowly down one cheek. He'd made her cry? Was that a happy cry? Her head shifted slightly to the right. A pit formed in his gut. Uh-oh. She began to shake, and her head rattled side-to-side as she clutched his hand and squeezed. The pit turned to cement.

"I . . . can't."

Chapter Eleven

Six years later

There had never been a time in Caroline's life when she knew she belonged. Nor had she figured out her purpose—if she had one. She suddenly felt nostalgic as she remembered a time when a friend had suggested this was one of the three essentials of life. A purpose—wasn't everyone supposed to have one? Hell, she didn't even have a good handle on a career. She'd roamed the world seeking her *big story* only to return broke and lonely, still an outsider in a world that wasn't her own. Now, she was partner to her friend Abigail's dream.

She was fairly used to the unsettled pocket in the pit of her stomach. She glanced around the florist business Abby had enticed her to join. Plants. Flowers. Loads of boxes waiting for her to open and place stock on shelves. Admittedly, the place felt nice, but not completely *right*. At least not for her.

Was it totally nuts to want more?

Abby's phone rattled to life on the counter where she'd left it, and Caroline couldn't resist a glance at the screen. A text message. Too funny. The idiot guy who'd started texting Abby in error was now *group texting* her and several others. "You might want to get that, Abs. They're talking about you."

The whole thing was drop-dead-roll-on-the-floor hilarious. Out of nowhere, the guy had started texting her by mistake, and Abby was in a tizzy 24–7.

Caroline hadn't been much help since she'd actually started the whole mistaken-identity crisis. When the guy randomly texted Abby, Caroline thought it would be funny to fire off a response from Abby's phone. Unfortunately, it prompted a slew of further texting that cast Abby as the alter ego of the man's friend. Now, the texting had gone on for days, and Abby was completely flustered about what to do. It wasn't *entirely* Caroline's fault: Abby had actually responded to one message and agreed to meet the guy—as the friend, of course.

Another text popped on her cell along with the accompanying buzz.

When Abby didn't respond, Caroline snapped up the phone. "Holy shit!" Caroline's eyes were glued to the texts. "Did you see these group messages?"

"Some of them. Hey, I thought you said I needed to stop spying and set him straight."

It was bad enough that the guy had confused her number with a friends'. Now he was adding her to his *group* messages. Caroline lowered her voice to make it mocking and masculine. "There really is a running chick? Yeah, nearly killed her with the neighbor's dog. You weren't with the neighbor? No, just helping with the dog. Good. No warts? No, she's nice. Seeing her again? Already did. Twice. Damn, that was fast." She read the screen out loud then slapped a hand to the counter and giggled. Apparently the guy had knocked some innocent jogger down with his dog then tried to ask her out. What a dork. Wait—holy crap. The jogger had been Abby! "This is the same guy you met while out running?" Well, the guy was original, if not smooth.

Another text message buzzed, and Caroline read the screen. "You know one of these guys is a real jerk. He said, 'So the tits *are* real?'"

"What! He did not!" Abby ran to her side and peered over her shoulder. Caroline felt the tenseness in her friend's body. "I thought you were joking."

"Nope. It gets worse. Look." Caroline handed over the phone, and Abby read the others. Her expression darkened to a thunderstorm complete with lightning bolts.

Fifteen minutes later, Caroline was clipping along the sidewalk headed to her first investigative assignment since she'd ditched her contract reporter gig. The idiot guy and his friends were meeting for lunch, and she planned to crash their fun and perhaps uncoil the knot of confusion she'd caused Abby. Or maybe just to ID the asshole and see if he was worth the effort. Besides, no one said smack about her friends and lived to laugh.

Inside the restaurant, she scoured the room and found a table of four guys that fit the general description. She planted herself in the next available booth—which happened to be right beside them. With her back to the group, she emptied her tray onto the table, spread out her food, and took a bite.

I'll just snap a few pictures with my phone and send them back for her to see who she's been texting. Caroline lifted her phone, put her tongue out, and focused. *Snap.*

She looked at the photo. Ugh. Worst selfie *ever*. She looked awful. Delete. *One more with little of me and lots of four delicious guys in the background.* Lifting the phone again, she focused, did her best pucker-up look, and—*snap.*

Holy crap. Did that guy just photobomb me? No way. She slammed the phone down and grabbed her fork. *Busted.* She shoved her salad around the plate a couple times and slipped a small scoop of chicken through her lips. Yum. At least they'd picked a good place to eat.

The discussion matter in the booth next to her was typical guy stuff, mostly about baseball—but then the conversation shifted. How do guys do that? They start out talking business or sports then in a nanosecond switch to women. And the woman in question just happened to be her best friend. At least the guy was decent looking and a lot better in person. She had to admire the way he avoided the slew of questions thrown his way about the *runner chick. Abby would be so pissed if she knew they'd spent three whole minutes talking about her boobs.*

Caroline turned the phone over in her lap and glanced across a shoulder. They couldn't see what she was doing. She thumbed through her pictures and looked at the last photo. Oh, God. He *had* photobombed her. She zoomed in on the dorky face and felt a sense of familiarity.

Wait.

Was that Roger Freeman? He *looked* like the goofball she'd dated. In an older, more mature way. That was years ago, so who would know? *He's flaring his nostrils and giving you the crazy eyes, girl.* Obviously *not* mature.

Yeah, had to be him.

This little investigative excursion was officially over. Caroline grabbed her empty drink glass and scooted out of the booth. She'd get a quick refill and hit the road. The uneaten food caused a tiny gurgle of regret for leaving such a great meal. It was a crime to walk away from that chicken. She grabbed a wing and took one last bite. With her napkin and purse in one hand, she carried her drink to the soda fountain.

A flood of memories wafted over her, causing a slight chill. She shivered. All the bad choices and wrong decisions she'd ever made had returned to haunt her. From the corner of her eye, she noted that Roger had climbed out of the booth and was headed her way.

Don't look. Do. Not. Even. Raise your head. She slapped a lid on her drink, gathered her things, and turned to leave. Was he staring? Caroline smelled that familiar Polo scent. She wanted to get a quick close-up, but she just couldn't force herself. Had he recognized her? God, she hoped not.

Just put one foot in front of the other and go. She stepped away and pushed out of the restaurant, disappointed that she'd left a perfectly good plate of food behind. Skipping meals was normal under their new work schedule, but doing so just to avoid a confrontation was sad.

Surely, it wasn't Roger. He would have said something. It wasn't possible he'd let an opportunity to blast her failure go without a word. After all, he'd tried to join her. He'd made all sorts of attempts to get her to take him along to help with the photos and brainstorm her ideas. *Two minds were better than one,* he'd said. Surely he'd love to know how right he'd been? How fabulously she had failed?

Chapter Twelve

Roger stared after the spiked-haired version of Caroline. Had she recognized him? She'd barely glanced his way. Nope. Wow. Had he really become a forgotten memory?

Of course he had, and why not? They'd only been together a short while, and not once during that time had she ever given him any indication it would last past graduation. She'd fully intended to follow in her nonexistent father's footsteps and pursue a journalistic career. Which was why Roger had only tried to talk her out of leaving once. Okay, maybe twice, but that was out of desperation—aided by double-shots of Jägermeister. Despite his last-ditch effort, she wouldn't be swayed.

It was wrong to expect her to give up a dream so big. Thank God she hadn't allowed him to derail her, though it still burned that she kept him from tagging along. Had it worked out for her?

He went back to the booth and slid in across from his best friend, Carter, who gave him a look. "Take a picture next time, it lasts longer," Carter said.

Roger slipped the lid from his tea and added a dose of sweetener. "I think I know her."

"Then you should have said something."

"I'm not sure," he lied. "The hair's different, and she didn't recognize me." It was most definitely Caroline—but she had moved on.

Unlike him. He had tanked. Stalled permanently. He had done as his father demanded, dropping several classes and taking on a full-time job to help his mother with bills. As a result, his graduation was derailed for almost a year. Still, the job had helped him get his foot in the door at the legal firm, which he later joined. They even helped him with his remaining education.

Back in his office after lunch, he opened the door of his credenza and pulled out the camera. Her note was underneath a pile of pictures he'd taken. She'd left it on the window of his Land Rover. That was all he'd been worth at the time, a fricking note. He read it for the gazillionth time.

Roger,

You have to be HERE, and I can't stay. It would be wrong for you to go when there are so many people here who need you. It would be wrong for me to stay and not at least TRY to be a journalist.

Caro

No love you, no XOXO—nothing. Bland and impersonal. Screw that.

His office was lined with more pictures he'd taken since. "At least I learned how to use the fancy camera Mom and Dad bought me. Caroline taught me one thing worth keeping. The rest was shit."

"What was shit?" Carter leaned against the doorframe.

Did I say that out loud?

Roger shrugged. "Nothing. My parents bought me this for my birthday the year I graduated from high school. It took me three years and a tutor to learn all the fancy buttons."

Carter waved a hand at the framed photos adorning his walls. "You took all these with that?"

He nodded. "Most of them. Yes."

"Wow, I assumed you'd bought them. Why haven't you told me anything about this? You have a talent, man. I thought the only thing you could do well was shoot your mouth off. What d'ya know—you can shoot other things, too."

Smartass. "Yeah, yeah—you're a real wisenheimer. Photography doesn't exactly equate to talent. Anyone can use a camera, after all." Roger set the camera back over the other prints, hoping Carter wouldn't see the envelope below.

"Not anyone and everyone has such an eye for turning it into art. All I ever use is my phone camera to take pictures, and those are nothing like these. These are awesome. You could sell them. I should hire you to take pics for my place." Carter had an apartment in a swanky part of town.

"Who would buy them? I have a stash of pictures you can go through. If you like any, they're yours. We'd just need to blow them up and add a frame."

Carter raised his brows like someone had just handed him a plate of filet mignon. "Really? Awesome. I'm serious, though. You're always complaining about how much money you don't have—and the answer's staring you in the face, bro. If I were Jackson, I'd say it was karma or some other kind of holistic shit he's always preaching, but in this case, he'd be right. Besides, it doesn't cost anything to try. There're all sorts of websites for uploading photos."

Roger's phone sounded and Carter took the ring as his cue to leave. Roger grabbed the phone, intent on blocking Caroline from his mind.

His mother checking in certainly helped. Nothing worked better to ruin a fantasy than listening to her drone on. "Have you had a chance to deposit the check for this month? I'm sorry to ask, but things are kind of tough right now."

Roger had been depositing checks for his mother since the spring of his senior year in college. He thanked his dad for that responsibility, though she was as much to blame. Ruth was a brilliant woman, salutatorian of her graduating class, yet she'd never had the courage to pursue a worthy job. Instead, she'd taken on office jobs that allowed her to work a minimal schedule and be at home for the family. She could have done much more, but for some reason she didn't seem to believe it. Perhaps she felt undeserving?

Her financial needs grew more desperate once his father decided it was time for him to remarry. Apparently a new wife and wedding stretched his father's income too much. So Roger had taken a longer than normal path through college in order to help his family out. It was his heritage, his responsibility— his transcendence into manhood. Pay bills. Work hard. Support yourself. That's what a man does, according to dear old dad. What was so great about being a man?

The fraternity had been an unnecessary extravagance, but his mother thought he needed stability along with "social graces" and a "brotherly influence." Roger preferred solitude and quiet, but he appeased his parents and did the legacy stint. In truth, he'd simply done what was expected of him, as he'd done all his life. Still, his brothers had been a big plus in getting his legal job, and that had been a career-starter.

His father could have waited another year before collapsing. It would have allowed him to finish school before he had to funnel money to his mother. Who knows? He might have even accompanied Caroline to Europe and taken a completely different path. The jury was still out as to whether that was a blessing or curse.

Roger stared out the window. The clouds had settled in cauliflower bunches with darkened edges that threatened a storm. He glanced back at the photos on his desk. A small roll of thunder reminded him of his mother's question. "No, sorry, I haven't had a chance. I'll log onto the bank account and transfer funds this evening. How's everything else going? Is Rebecca enjoying her sophomore year?" His sister had enrolled in a nearby junior college as a freshman then transferred to U of H once she'd gained some credits. Thankfully she hadn't pledged because Roger knew his father was only sending a pittance to help with costs. The rest was spread between himself and Rhianna, who'd recently gotten married.

"She wants to quit."

"No way."

"Yes way. You should talk to her. She says it's a waste of time, that she already knows most of what they're teaching."

"Of course she says that; she's a sophomore. The first year is always a review, a test to see where you stand. It won't be so easy from here on."

"Apparently she doesn't agree. She thinks she'd be more useful by getting a job."

His mother had a point. Rebecca was borderline psychotic when it came to studying, and she'd always been the top of the class in everything. It wasn't enough to be smart; she had to be *smarter* than the rest. Still, the education was necessary if she wanted to have a decent future. "I'll call her this weekend. Everything else okay?"

Ruth coughed into the phone. Roger reared back and looked at the phone as if expecting phlegm to burst through the airwaves. A few ticks of silence. "Eric and Patty stopped by yesterday."

Oh. *That* was the real reason she'd called. His father and the new wife—who wasn't all that new anymore. He wasn't sure what to say. "Why?"

"Um. They wanted me to be the first to know they're *pregnant*." His mother's voice dripped sarcasm. And pain.

Roger slammed a hand to his desk. "What? Are you serious?"

"As a heart attack. Apparently they were worried I would have a problem with it. I mean, why shouldn't I? Hell, who *doesn't* have a problem with their spouse leaving them for a near-teenager after twenty years and four children? He leaves me scraping for money and everything else, and I'm supposed to be *happy* he's finally *found* himself. Hell, I just want to know at what point he *lost* himself."

There she went again. He hated the rants. After six years, one would expect her to move on with her life—or at least get one. "Mom."

A few more ticks on the phone. "Sorry."

He couldn't blame her for her bitter attitude toward his dad. He had similar thoughts—but just didn't have time to allow them to fester. "No worries. I'll call Rebecca. Check your account later today, okay? I'm sorry, but I have to get back to work."

"You'll come by this weekend?"

Spending agonizing minutes hearing the gory details about Eric's new family and her feelings about them appealed to him about as much as yanking out his toenails. "Of course."

Roger was nothing if not dependable. He flipped through the pictures on his desk and shrugged. Carter had a point. He might as well *try* making a little cash off his expensive hobby.

A few weeks later, while sitting at his desk and sipping his coffee, Roger caught a glimpse of bright purple move past his door. He darted a glance down the hallway but saw nothing. A few minutes later, a soft tapping came at the door. "Excuse me, I'm here to water the plants."

Caroline?

It really was her. He had plants? Roger glanced around the room and spotted a tuft of green leaves that spilled over a pot near the window. Wow, when did that happen? Carter had mentioned getting foliage for the office, but Roger hadn't expected any for himself. "Uh, okay."

A purple scarf tied loosely at her neck draped over her pert and graceful shoulders. He had always loved Caroline's shoulders. Though slightly shorter than average, she held herself tall and kept her back straight, which made them stand out—especially in strapless or sleeveless clothes. Today, she wore a black sleeveless blouse over a black and white checkered skirt. Black tights covered her legs.

Roger couldn't recall ever seeing her in a dress other than the casual skirt that she'd thrown over her swimsuit. That entire day was carved into his memory. He glanced at the spiked heels of her ankle-high boots. Definitely had never seen her in heels. Warmth sprinted through his chest and did a cartwheel in his lower parts.

She searched the room, met his gaze briefly, then found her target and strode to the lone plant. She doused it generously and plucked off a couple dead leaves. Without a word, she turned. Her footsteps pounded like tennis balls on the carpet toward the door. Was he that easy to forget? "You look great, Caro."

He'd used the nickname intentionally. Her water can tapped against the door, and he heard a soft gasp. Her head turned slightly. But she didn't meet his searching gaze. *Turn around. Come on. Acknowledge.*

She yanked the door open and rushed out. He grinned at his computer and picked up the contract he'd been reviewing. The warmth of the storm in his stomach spread. She remembered. Now what?

Chapter Thirteen

Caroline pulled at the hem of her skirt and continued down the hall. Why had Abby decided to take on corporate clients and do plant maintenance? More importantly, why had fate chosen *this* client?

What were the odds of Roger being there? A deluge of memories clouded her brain, both good and bad. She rushed through the remaining maintenance work and escaped the building.

Why had the powers-that-be decided to throw him in her path? Come on. She'd spent the last few years healing from her bad choices, and he was the last thing she needed. One of the worst choices she'd made, second only to the screw-up in Teslehad.

Her arm still tingled from the wound that put her in the hospital that day. She rubbed the ache and accidentally tripped over a ridge in the sidewalk. Shivers scrambled up her spine and settled into the perpetual knot that tightened her shoulders. She'd watched six children die on the street in Teslehad, something no one should see. She had done nothing.

Correction: Her presence caused the whole incident. Those sick bastards had wanted to make a statement, and then she'd done as expected and written about it. But hell, that was worth nothing to those kids or their families. They were still rotting in a shared grave dug into a hillside.

"Are you searching for ghosts, Caroline?" Abby's voice startled her back to the present.

The chill rolled farther into a good, stiff headache. She growled. "Actually, in a way, yes. I need to *leave*."

Abby opened her mouth to tease, but after Caroline gave her a nasty grimace, she clamped her lips shut. She nodded sympathetically and motioned toward the door, but Caroline was already on her way. That was the one thing Caroline adored about Abby: the woman knew when to shut up and let her work through the demons of her past. She also knew better than to ask about them, which was another huge plus. Abby had known her before the shit-storm and sensed that something had changed inside her, but she'd never pushed for details.

Unlike Caroline's mother, God rest her soul, who was never one to allow a good story to disappear into history. Nope, before she passed, her mother would poke and poke until she'd unraveled all her daughter's pain and stress. So many psychiatrists had evaluated her over the years that she fancied herself an amateur counselor. For Caroline, this normally resulted in even more hurt. At least her mother hadn't lived to see the hell she was going through now—trying to fend off her questions and accusations would have been unbearable.

If her mother had mentioned she was ill, Caroline probably wouldn't have even been *there* in Teslehad on that horrible day. She would have stayed to nurse her mother back to health, and all those kids would have lived. Which is probably why her mother kept silent: she was the biggest supporter of her daughter's ridiculous dream.

Or would they have? The knot tangled further, and Caroline's head throbbed. No, they'd have died without a single witness, their tiny little bodies piled over each other like rag dolls, discarded and forgotten. Instead they had a rookie journalist who freaked out. She finally wrote the story and sent it off. Then ran like hell to try forgetting their hollow eyes watching her in death.

Oh God.

She rushed back to the shop, synced her iPod to the stereo, and blasted Coldplay over the speakers. It wasn't until she noticed a customer shouting to their friend as they admired an arrangement that she realized she'd cranked it up twice. Oops.

She turned the sound down as the woman's voice screeched, "You should have them hold your husband's hand, and maybe you won't get a fishing vest next year for your anniversary."

Her words echoed across the store—along with the giggles of her friend, who nodded. "Mine bought me a washer. He remembered that ours was broken and thought I'd appreciate it—not exactly romantic to buy something that you know needs work. A spa treatment or night out would have been a little more fun. Hell, even a sexy gown with a bunch of these roses." The woman flicked a hand over a vase of pink and red.

Caroline had heard these phrases a zillion times from women who wished their husbands were more romantic. And yet those very same husbands came in once in a while and bought these arrangements on their way home. It seemed awfully romantic to someone who had no one bringing anything home at all. Not even a washer or vacuum cleaner.

The woman smiled and redeemed herself. "Actually, it's not fair for me to say that—he buys flowers a lot. He's hopelessly romantic, but they're always a day or two late because he forgets."

An idea zapped Caroline. She'd badgered Abby to let her do some advertisements for the store and tinkered with a blog post. *That's it!* She shoved her scarier memories into the closets of her brain and starting working on a blog ad, punching the keys of the computer between helping customers. At least she could put her journalism degree to use in a way that didn't haunt her when she hit the sheets at night. Her head was glued to the screen when Abby returned and delved into the back office to do the bookkeeping. It wasn't until Abby returned to nix the lights that Caroline let herself relax and ease back into the cozy fragrance of the store. She'd immersed herself in the lighthearted blogging and advertisement efforts enough to banish her nightmares, at least for now.

She looked down at the striped leggings she'd worn to work. In a whimsical fashion, they ushered away the tenseness in her body.

She'd always had a thing for fun colors. The leggings were bright, cheerful, and so *not* the drab green and tan camo she'd worn while trekking across Europe. Thank God.

The door to the store jingled, and she turned to acknowledge the new guest. "Welcome to—Oh…Dad."

"Hi there." Bob Sanders gave a sheepish grin and shrugged with hands extended, acknowledging her disappointment. She hadn't quite adjusted to having him back in her life after all the years he'd been searching out stories for the *New York Times*.

It took her mother's catastrophic illness and the associated family drama to bring him home to stay. Still, somehow they'd managed to piece a strange but comfortable relationship together from the catacombs of silence. Theirs was a love-hate relationship—or maybe it was hate-love. She hated him for missing her childhood. She loved him for coming back when her mother was ill and never leaving her side. It was odder than odd, but she'd be a fool to complain and lose them both.

And why was he still here? Her mother's illness had taken a bad turn right after the big blow-up in Teslehad, which gave Caroline a convenient excuse to come home. Thankfully she'd never had a chance to tell her about that day, though she was still angry her mother hadn't divulged the illness before she left.

"Feel like joining an old man for dinner?" Her father was sixty going on forty-five. He still drew glances from the older women, but he was oblivious. Caroline found it odd considering he'd so rarely been around his wife. It seemed unlikely he could be that devoted. He wasn't gay either—she'd seen the pile of girly magazines hidden in his closet. He must simply be ambivalent about women, she thought.

Caroline stared out the window. "I finally finished that boring book you wrote." He'd given her a copy of his life's work—a story about the many Korean War veterans who had fallen through the cracks of the system and disappeared into lives of trouble and desperation. It was his obsession.

"I'm guessing you slept through most of it." He moved closer as the door jingled closed. Her father wasn't a towering man, but he held himself well and stayed fit. His hair was the color of tree bark, and his eyes a cloudy blue. Caroline was glad she'd inherited her mother's eyes. Still blue, but sharper—crisp. Clear and honest.

"Not really. It was…interesting. How'd you end up with that assignment anyway?"

He shrugged. Abby doused the remaining lights and ushered them toward the door. He waited for Caroline to gather her bag. "A family thing. Your mother's dad served, and he was—"

"Killed. I know."

"Yes, well, not exactly….Sometimes things aren't always what they seem. So, what'd you think of my stories?"

Should she admit that she'd had to put the book down because too many painful memories rushed through as she read? Recent memories of her own experiences with losing her mother.

She gave a vague answer as they strolled to his car outside and drove to dinner. Her father was a creature of habit, eating at the same dive a few blocks from his house two or three times a week. The place served crazy foods like sausage and spaetzle quiche, and their recipes were filled with flour, salt, and enough carbs to wallpaper Fort Knox. A heart surgeon's nightmare.

It wasn't until they'd finished their meal and were waiting on the check that Caroline noticed the manila folder he'd tucked under a leg. Had he brought it with him? He opened the clasp and reached inside to pull something from within. The papers he tossed in front of her slid to a stop with a solid hiss. Pictures.

Caroline focused on the images of the glossy photo stock. They were eerily similar to ones she wished to forget. She blinked and shifted her gaze to his eyes. "You took these?"

He nodded. "Yep, but not these." He tossed a couple more photos that sprawled haphazardly over the first. She recognized them as ones she'd taken of locals in Teslehad. He tapped each print. "They're good."

Caroline's throat closed. The compliment of her work loomed between them but mattered little—she still couldn't look at them. The staccato sound of gunfire burned her ears as memories flooded through the concrete dam she'd tried to build around her thoughts. Why had he brought them? And where had he found them? "I hate them."

He picked his teeth with a toothpick he'd sweet-talked the waitress to provide. When satisfied with the result, he flicked his tongue across the veneers the dentist had recently put over his failing teeth. He still had trouble speaking. "Understood. I hated mine, too—at first."

"What do you mean, at first?"

He shrugged. "Caroline, I read about what happened that day."

"How? The article was never published. I made them promise not to. I—"

"My seniority has a few perks sometimes, or *had* at one time. After you pulled back your submission, the editor sent me an email attached with your draft and the pictures. He wanted me to encourage you."

A weight of lead sunk further into her chest. He'd read her rant? Her throat turned to a crusted cavern that no words could pass through.

Her father pulled out another picture and tossed it forward. She knew it well. A small child with his arms closed over another in a failed attempt to protect. His sister was only a tiny fragment of his size. He'd done the best he could to cover her and take the blows of the gunshots, but the end result was fatal for both children. He'd tried so hard to wrap her up like a tiny doll in his arms.

Evil had a way of seeping through the best of packages and spoiling the contents. They had both died despite the good brother's efforts. Caroline had felt the boiling surge of anger that day for the first time. It rose from deep within her, daring her to lash out at the injustice. But she had been too much of a coward. "I should have done something."

Her father frowned. Was he disappointed in her, too? "What could you have done differently?"

She had no idea. "Anything. Something. They were children. They weren't involved in what was happening over there. It was a war they hadn't started and couldn't fight."

"True." The check came; her father snatched it up and dug out his wallet.

"It wasn't even a war, Dad. It was a skirmish—something that hadn't even made the news here. It was like they'd never existed." She choked on the last word. Hell, that was what had bothered her most.

After dropping a few bills on top of the check, her father held the picture in front of Caroline's eyes. She met his gaze rather than stare at the lifeless bodies. He tsked. "They did exist. And because you were there to take this photograph, their sacrifice was recorded. That's what journalists do. You couldn't have stopped it, and had you tried, you would have been in the same grave. *Then* no one would have known. Honey, there was nothing you could have done and lived to tell."

He was wrong. "I was a journalist—I was protected." He knew they had safe passage—he'd scoffed at the Geneva Convention in his publications for years.

He cursed. "You think anyone doing *that*," he tapped a finger on the pile of photos, "cares whether you have journalistic free passage? I know you're not stupid. They would have killed you, buried you with those kids, and slept like logs afterward. Another journalist missing in a foreign country, presumed lost. Come on, you knew it too. You did your job—and you did the right thing."

"I did nothing."

"You told the story."

A knife seared through her heart. "No, I didn't. I was afraid, and as soon as I hit native soil, I warehoused the story and came running home to hide. Face it, Dad, I'm not a journalist. Not even close. I'm not like you. I can't handle the death and brutality day after day. I want to shoot every damn one of those baby killers. And I don't even own a gun."

He slapped a hand on the table and slid to a stand. "You don't need a gun. You have a camera and a brain. You ready to go?"

She nodded. Once they were back in his car, he laid a hand on hers. "I hate to tell you this, honey, but other than the fact you look more like your mother, you're exactly like me. By the way, I liked hearing you call me Dad. You can do that more often if you want."

They changed the subject before he dropped her off. She was thankful for the company and a chance to talk about anything that kept her mind off her ghosts. She wished he hadn't delved into the painful memories. Why was it soothing to know he had ghosts of his own? That was borderline sick. She shook the thought away. There was one truly great thing about her new life: the serenity of knowing the worst thing she'd ever deal with was a grumbling customer or a late shipment.

Not death.

Chapter Fourteen

Roger shifted on his couch and blinked at the glow of his laptop screen. *Was that dollar amount real? Holy shit.* The website showed an income—*an income*—from the slew of pictures he'd uploaded. Carter was right, but he'd never tell him. To top it off, the money was automatically deposited in his bank account. He pumped his fist in a tiny celebration. "Yes."

A soft whimper forced him to change focus. He'd been wrestling with finances and work projects for too long. He glanced at the gray whiskers and clouded eyes of his old friend. "Hey, Conan. You need to go out, buddy?"

Ruff. That was affirmative.

Roger grabbed the leash and waited as the dog lumbered toward the door. Eventually he'd need to accept the inevitable and take the fateful visit to the vet. Not today. Or anytime soon. He couldn't handle such a monumental decision. Besides, as long as Conan could walk, Roger wasn't cutting his time on earth short. It was wrong.

Outside, the dog maneuvered down the ramp Roger had added when the steps became too difficult. It had taken only a few times for Conan to realize the ramp was his. He was a smart dog. Old, but not stupid. *I'm gonna cry like a baby when he dies.*

A cool breeze scattered leaves across the sidewalk. Roger dropped to sit on the steps while the dog shuffled around the same territory he'd marked earlier in the day. Heaven forbid another dog try to take over his yard; it'd take all night for him to repair the damage.

Roger's cell jolted into action inside the house, and he jumped up to answer. Conan lifted his head, drool dribbling from his chin into the grass. Roger glanced at the screen and debated answering.

History proved that not answering his mother didn't deter her efforts, and that she'd just call again in a few minutes. He turned off the volume, grabbed a glass of water, and returned to the peacefulness of his front step.

Fifteen minutes later, the sound of tires crunching on the loose pavement of his driveway woke him from a daydream. He really needed to get the driveway fixed, but he liked its dual functionality. It gave him advance warning of pending confrontation. Ahem, company. He grimaced at the silhouette of his mother in her aging Buick.

"Why don't you answer your phone, son?"

He shrugged. "It's inside."

Conan glanced at Ruth, sighed, and lumbered up the ramp to wait by the door. He was thrilled to see her, too.

Tap. Tap. Tap. Tap. Were those heels on the sidewalk? His mother seldom wore heels; they hurt her corns. Her feet came into view. Nope. Sneakers. Still, the clatter continued.

Where was it coming from? Ruth jogged toward him. "I wanted to warn you, but I didn't get here quite fast enough. Remember that young lady, Marina, that I mentioned meeting at the vet? The one who's a decorator? I told her to come by and take a look—it's on me." A decorator for his house? The thought was laughable. On her? Yeah right.

Oh, hell, just shoot me. He'd told her not to ever try matchmaking him again, and damned if she hadn't ignored his words. His mother meant well but was always seeking a "suitable" woman who had as much personality as a piece of grass in the winter.

A sharp growl came from behind, and Roger rose to his feet and pushed the door open for Conan. "*Now*? You told her to come by today? Mom, I can't—I have plans." Actually, he had a blank slate but wasn't telling her.

"Oh, sorry. You can just let her in, and she'll take a look, and then you guys can get together later to go over her ideas, right?

Maybe one night this week." Ruth reeked of hopeful conniving and fake pleasantries. There was no way in hell he'd let a random woman peruse his apartment. Not happening.

Tap. Tap. "Hi there!" Marina called out. Stilettoes, twiggy legs, and a too-short skirt rounded his mother's vehicle, and Roger shut his mouth as the sleek and shiny woman approached. "Thanks for letting me stop by. I'm so excited about this project. I haven't done a bachelor's place in a long time."

Today wouldn't bring an end to his dry spell, either. He forced himself to smile. "Um, I'm not really prepared for company…I'm leaving in a bit." He tried to think of somewhere to go. Maybe over to Carter's to watch the game. The Astros played at one. "I can't afford—"

Marina waved a manicured hand. "Don't worry about it. Our parents go way back, and it's on me."

"I'm not a charity case either."

Her eyes flared defensively. "I didn't mean…I wasn't saying you were. It's just…your mom thought we should meet."

"My mother thought? Really? She can think for herself, not me, and I'll do the same." Roger yanked the door open and retreated inside. Their hushed murmurs sounded like static as he slammed the screen shut. Marina and his mother weren't deterred by his gruffness—they simply followed him inside. What to do? He wasn't in the mood for a fight. He just needed peace and quiet. Roger plodded out of the living room to his bedroom and clunked the door closed. He twisted the lock into place and grabbed a book from his bedside. Perhaps they'd leave if he hid out long enough.

The rattling and grinding of chatter in the main rooms annoyed him so much, he slammed the book shut, grabbed his keys, and headed back outside. After stowing Conan in the vehicle, he thrust the car in reverse and wheeled away from the house. Whatever happened to *a man's home is his castle*?

The phrase was obviously made famous by a man who didn't have an overbearing mother and a bevy of sisters. Without a destination, Roger found himself standing on a pier overlooking Thompson Lake. A few years earlier, Conan wore out the lake's beach chasing Frisbees and seagulls. Now, the dog only plodded to the water's edge and soaked his feet.

God, I need a break. A vacation from this massive load of responsibilities, family, work—crap…everything.

Conan yelped. Roger searched the beach. Where'd he go? He was here a second ago with his feet in the water. The big guy was too old to swim and too slow to run far. Roger rotated. Twenty yards down the froth of water, the dog was tangled…in seaweed.

Even a trip to the shore wasn't without peril. Roger worked the dog's legs free and took him home. On his front door was a sticky note that appeared to be from his home office desk. Had they rummaged through his things? He grimaced.

Let's meet Thursday eight p.m. at Flannigan's Brewhouse to discuss my thoughts for your spaces. Thanks so much for the opportunity—see you there!

His nastiness hadn't deterred the woman one bit. No signature and no phone number to cancel either. Great.

Chapter Fifteen

Caroline learned that Roger worked with Abby's heartthrob the hard way. Abby and Caroline decided to take turns doing plant maintenance at their office after Abby talked the text-o-hunk, Carter into paying them to install and maintain plants for their building.

Caroline nearly bulldozed Roger outside the bathroom of their office. She feigned ignorance and apologized politely as if he were any other stranger, not looking him in the face. But he wasn't.

Caroline had been mildly surprised to learn about Roger's suspicion that Abby's voluptuous curves were medically induced. She hadn't remembered him being so snide or judgmental when they were in college. People change. God knows she had.

She wasn't shocked that he'd finished school and now managed projects like the one Carter was involved with. He'd always seemed the type to do big things.

At their shop, she plucked a broken stem from a pot of dahlias and stuck a fertilizer stick near the base. Touching the dirt, she decided it wasn't necessary to add water yet. The click of computer keys at the counter signified Abby's bookkeeping efforts were in full force. Abby had been tied up in knots for weeks over the texting confusion. Caroline would have sympathized if not for the fact that she kept making it worse by continuing the charade. The sound stopped for a second, and Abby sighed. "You know, I can't keep doing this."

"What?"

"Texting, chatting, all the deception. It's wrong."

"You're right. It's wrong." Caroline admitted.

"If I tell Carter, he'll hate me." Abby was obviously wrestling with her conscience. "Look how upset he got about me sleeping with Jackson."

Caroline spun around. "You slept with Jackson?"

"God, no. But when they made that snide remark about my chest, I fired off a response…and…well, Carter thought it was from him. It kind-of inferred that I had."

Caroline frowned. "Oh. You need to be careful how you phrase that, or a customer might get the wrong impression."

Abby plucked a pen from behind her ear and wrote something on a notepad. "What's worse? Pretending that it actually happened in order to *not* hurt him and lying—or actually doing it?"

The door whisked open and the FedEx deliveryman, in tight shorts and a crisp white shirt, rolled through with boxes for the store.

Caroline plopped a hand to her hip and gave her a skeptical frown. "You're kidding right? You know, for a guy who seemed so much fun in the beginning he sure gets riled up about stuff."

When the packages were signed for, Caroline pulled the paperwork and tossed it on the counter to add to Abby's records. Abby sighed. "I can't exactly fault the guy for having a problem with his best friend sleeping with his girl. That'd be like me going after one of your boyfriends."

She had a point. Caroline lifted one of the packages and shot her a snarky grin. "Seriously? We don't shop in the same supermarket when it comes to men, girl. I doubt that'd ever be an issue."

"Good point."

Caroline shifted the package to her hip, grabbed the other one and took them to the stock room. She unpacked the contents and started toward the front. "Say, you think we could make requests on who delivers the FedEx packages? That guy was seriously—Oh."

When the hell had Roger walked into the store? Had he heard her comment?

"Caroline." He nodded.

"Dickwad," she acknowledged.

"Hey, he's a customer!" Abby retorted.

Okay, it wasn't exactly a customer-friendly response, but it was *Roger*. Why bother.

"You've changed, Caroline."

She forced her face to remain calm. "Yeah, well people usually do when they get older."

Roger coughed. "I didn't say it was *bad*, just different."

Abby's eyes volleyed from Roger to Caroline as she absorbed the conversation. "You guys know each other?"

Roger nodded. "Sort of. Ask her. We, uh, hung out in college a while before Caroline ran off to find herself."

His voice seeped sarcasm, and for some reason it tilted Caroline over the edge. "I didn't *run off*, and I certainly wasn't looking for myself in the process. I was pursuing my career, *remember*? I'm a journalist. I mean, I *was* a journalist."

After a volley of choice words between the two, Roger stomped toward the door and yanked it open. He stared at her for a heartbeat. "God, you're angry. Did your hair start spiking up like that when your personality began bristling too? Or is that something you caught over in Germany or Scotland, like the foot and mouth disease they had in 2001?"

That was it. Caroline rattled off a couple of f-bombs along with some other fancy phrases and stormed to the stock room. If she stayed in the vicinity of Roger for one more minute, she'd— she'd—punch him in the nose.

Retreat was safer. She unpacked boxes and applied price tags until her nerves calmed. She barely registered that Abby continued talking with him for a few minutes before he left.

"Soooo, Roger, that was interesting." Abby tapped a pen against the counter. "Can I help you with something?"

"As a matter of fact, yes." He strode to the counter, pulled his cell from his pocket and showed her the display. Since he was the one responsible for mixing up the numbers, he should have felt a little guilty about using it to his advantage. He didn't.

"Okay, you caught me."

She rattled on with all sorts of excuses and avoided his questions. Did she really think he believed her story? Roger walked outside when a customer interrupted. He watched through the window and waited until the person left, then called her cell. When Abby answered, he convinced her to meet him outside when the store closed. His intention of mixing the numbers was to get Abby and Carter together, not cause a freaking technology nightmare. The two of them were a disaster. Abby met him later, but after their conversation, things seemed even more convoluted than before. How the hell could he help Carter if Abby continued to add layers and layers of technology confusion?

He considered the dilemma on the way home. Hell, their communication issues weren't his problem. At least he'd tried. He hit road construction and sat for over twenty minutes while flashing lights and signs prevented his movement. The bright colors were almost as blaringly obnoxious as those striped leggings Caroline wore. His lips twitched, and he felt a smile stretch across his face in amusement. She'd changed all right, but the wild innocence and crazy bravado was still there. She had simply hidden it under all those crazy layers of fabric. And tons of misdirected anger.

It took him a few more stoplights, but he finally figured out how to handle the situation with Caroline. Reading her blog had made him realize how much he needed closure. To see if there was even a glimmer of a chance that they might be able to salvage something from the past. Or maybe he was a glutton for punishment. He called Abby and set up a time to meet. It was easy to bribe her into arranging a short sit-down with Caroline. After all, she was riddled with guilt over how to resolve things in her own relationship and practically overjoyed to focus on someone else' communication needs.

When Roger pulled into his drive, his cell bleeped a text. He glanced at the screen.

Hi there, Miranda here. It's Thursday. Are you still coming?

Oh shit.

He debated cancelling, but his mom would call in a few minutes if he dared—and he wasn't ready for another bashing session. Besides, Miranda was simply trying to do her job. You couldn't fault her for that.

He typed in a response and quickly let Conan out before jumping back into the car. He'd see what she wanted to do, then politely refuse her services and end the evening. He glanced at the clock on the dash. If he timed things well, he could get back in time to watch the Astros game at seven.

Flannigan's Brewhouse was a local favorite with most of his friends. Good food, lots of specials on draft beers, and decent feature bands on weekends. Thursday nights had become the favorite time for young bands to debut on the small stage. He'd never heard of the group playing this night, but he wasn't picky. He wasn't staying.

He'd taken four steps inside when a perfectly manicured set of nails wrapped around his wrist and yanked him onto the dance floor.

"Yay. You're here." Miranda's crazy-ass heels put her almost at eye level with him. The pile of curls she'd layered into a knot on her head gave her an extra inch. Scary.

"Yeah, I'm here, but I can't—"

The band kicked the volume up and his words were lost. *Stay.*

She grabbed his bicep and yelled a few undistinguishable words into his ear before bouncing up and down to the music.

It was actually pretty decent music, too. He figured he could dance to one or two songs before he left, just to be cordial. Twenty or so minutes later, he was sweating his ass off, and in desperate need of a drink. Fortunately the band stopped long enough for him to speak.

"I have to have something to drink or I'm going to pass out. You thirsty?"

She nodded and gave an order for a fancy martini he'd never heard of. He hoped he could remember the name long enough to order it. "I'll meet you at that table over there." Miranda pointed toward a dark corner, and he nodded.

At the bar, someone tapped Roger on the shoulder, and he turned to see his friend Jackson. "Who's the Vegas showgirl?"

Roger frowned. "No one." Maybe her clothes were a little flashy, but he wouldn't exactly call them stripper style.

Jackson lifted a finger to order a beer as Roger waited for their drinks. "Really? 'Cause she sure doesn't look like no one. Especially the way she was rubbing rusties with you."

Roger's beer arrived, and he took a swig. "Rusties?"

Jackson laughed. "Yeah, but I have a feeling they won't be rusty after tonight." He clicked his beer bottle to Roger's and strode back to his girlfriend, Amanda. *Very funny.*

Once the bartender finished Miranda's drink, Roger took it and worked his way toward the table. Why'd she pick one so dark and hidden…and right next to the band? There was no possible way he'd hear a word of her presentation. She bopped up and down on her stool like she was going to start dancing on it any second. He glanced around. She hadn't brought a presentation.

He leaned forward and spoke into her hair after she'd taken the drink. "So what do you think?"

She sipped her martini and yelled, "I think I want to dance some more." She yanked his free hand toward the floor. Roger desperately downed the remainder of his beer for hydration. What should he do? This obviously wasn't going to be a quick business meeting. In fact, based on their surroundings, he doubted she intended to talk shop at all.

So much for the game.

Two hours later, he trudged to his front door with Miranda close behind. Her fingers were tucked into his pocket and squeezing his backside. He should have rescheduled their meeting, but that would just mean another potential misunderstanding, and he wasn't up for it. Besides she said she wanted to *show* him her ideas. He was pretty sure he knew where that led.

He unlocked the door and shoved it wide for her to enter. Miranda stepped out of her heels, and suddenly he was looking four inches down at her pile of blonde frizz. With shoes in hand, she tiptoed into his house. Something about the swing of her hips and the way she rolled the shoes around in her fingers scared the hell out of him. Not because he expected she wanted to make use of his body, but because he wasn't sure he wanted hers. What the hell was wrong with him? He'd never been one to turn down getting laid before.

She rotated, dropped her shoes, and walked her fingers up his chest. "So, I thought we could do something really dark and sexy with this room."

He quirked a brow. "Like what?"

She leaned up and whispered, "Come here, and I'll show you."

Caroline surveyed the crowded shop and filled with pride. She couldn't stop smiling. Abby had nearly choked her to death by hugging the breath out of her when people started showing up to buy the new deal she'd advertised on her blog. The BFB package was the product of a little too much wine at a very late hour.

And it was brilliant, if she did say so herself.

BFB, Best Flower Budget, allowed busy and perhaps forgetful people to ensure they always remembered special occasions with an appropriate present. It was a subscription service for flowers and gifts. They'd sold half a dozen today, along with numerous other gifts and arrangements. She was exhausted by the time Abby finally closed up shop. The store was a disaster. As Caroline went to retrieve the cleaning supplies, she noticed she'd left the new deliveries unshelved. She tore open the boxes and tagged a beautiful set of crystal candleholders. They'd be a hit.

"Hey Gandhi. You have another customer." Abby called. Abby had coined Caroline's new nickname by prophesizing they'd turn a profit.

"Would you mind handling it? I'm in the middle of unpacking this delivery." She stared at one remaining box.

"I'll take the boxes for you. This one asked for you personally."

Huh? What? None of their customers knew her personally.

She dug out the dustpan and broom from a closet and used a hip to shove backward through the door just as Abby yanked it wide. She stumbled into the room. Oh, shit. "Roger?"

"What's up?"

She held up the broom. "Working." Abby shoved her in the back and closed the office door, flipping the lock in place. What the heck?

"I thought we should talk."

She heard the buzzer on the back door, then a clank. Abby had shoved her into the darkened store with Roger, then escaped out the back. The coward.

"What about? I mean, there's not much to say. We haven't exactly kept in touch." Her stomach did a small somersault, and she rubbed a hand down her front to still the rumble.

He stepped toward her. "Whose fault is that?"

Gulp. "Hey, I called."

He rolled his eyes. "How was it over there?"

Why did she have a sneaking feeling he already knew? "Fine. Good. What does it matter? That was years ago."

Roger stopped two feet away and shoved his hands in his pockets. "So, what's your story now?" He reached up and flipped a finger against her hair. "Have you turned into a man-hater, or is it just me that burns your ass?"

"It's just you," she snarked.

He snickered, exposing a glimpse of those famous dimples, then lifted a hand to run through his hair. "Well, that's a first."

"Oh come on. Not everyone thinks you're completely perfect."

That made him laugh once. "I'm not even close, and that wasn't what I meant. Most women hate me *after* they sleep with me. Not before. We never made it that far."

Caroline shrugged. "Well, there you have it then. I guess I just skipped to the punch line. Look at it this way: you dodged a bullet. 'Not before' insinuates there's an after coming. There isn't. That ship has already sailed, buddy."

Roger plucked a pink rose from a vase and held it to her cheek. His brown eyes twinkled in the dark. "Don't you ever wonder what we'd have been like together if we'd stuck it out?"

There was no way in hell she'd answer *that* question. She glanced beyond him as a police car's siren wailed past from the nearby station. The lights sent a blue comet across the room. "Stuck what out, Rog? We were friends. College buddies. It wasn't serious."

"Right." A flash of something crossed his face. Anger? Sadness? He held her gaze and eased closer until his lips hovered within inches. She tried to step backward, but her butt hit a shelf. Holding her breath, Caroline searched for an escape path. God knows her entire body had gone into overdrive as soon as he stepped into her comfort zone.

"Soooo, college buddy, how many guys have done this since me?" His lips felt warm and comfortable when they met hers. She stilled, trying not to respond.

She failed. Her brain fogged just enough to slow her response. She spoke against his lips. "You want a number or descriptions?"

His lip twitched at the corner as he trailed more kisses along her cheek before returning to her mouth. "I don't really care." His tongue flicked across her lips, and damned if her mouth didn't open without her consent.

He kissed her until her hand crawled up his chest and tickled through his thick brown hair. When he finally pulled away, her heart thudded against his chest. She gulped for air then spoke. "Would that be just the guys?"

He laughed, his heated breath toasting her face. "Very funny."

She shrugged in an attempt to get her pulse under control. "I thought so."

"Be serious, Caro."

Caroline frowned. "No. Let's don't. I hate serious." That was true. She'd had enough *serious* for a lifetime over in Teslehad. "I have no desire to be serious—not then, not now, not ever. So, if this little test of yours is over...can I go now?"

Chapter Sixteen

Three months later, Roger stared at the blackish-blue paint on his walls in bewilderment. Nothing about the changes felt right. How had he let Marina and his mother talk him into this? He snickered. *Because it was safer than meeting her for dinner a second time.* God knows what she'd do to him then. The giant marshmallow-shaped sectional dared him to jump aboard and toss the perfectly placed pillows. Wait. Was that a brown patch on the cushions? He stepped closer and crouched down to see…a paw. Conan was in that pile of pillows somewhere.

"Hey, big guy."

A moan echoed from the velour depths, and a pillow rumbled to life then shifted aside to reveal a chocolate eye surrounded in fur. Roger laughed. His bachelor-pad comfy couch was perfect for an oversized old bachelor—of the canine variety. Conan's head emerged from the pillows, and he arched a wrinkled ear to Roger as if to ask why he'd been roused from a perfect nap. The dog stretched, taking up all six feet of cushions, then rolled to display his back to Roger. A classic *leave me alone* move.

Roger obliged. He went to work.

Around nine o'clock, his mother called to remind him he was eating at her house on Saturday. At eleven thirty, Rhianna called to ask if he'd stop by and repair a broken hinge on her bathroom door. At 3:43, Rebecca texted to ask him a calculus question.

His life was run by women—and boring as hell. A slow boil in his brain seethed through and by the time he'd left the office, he'd snapped twice at the receptionist and said something incoherently inappropriate to Abby, the plant lady who just happened to be his friend Carter's soul mate. If he didn't get a little respite from overbearing female companionship, he was going to explode.

The fiasco with Rhianna's door increased his frustration exponentially. He showed up at her forty-year-old home wary of the time involved in her repair. His sister loved renovations. Truthfully, her friends were as much a project to her as her house: she was always trying to reinvent them into something more than they wished. Her husband, Trey, was no exception, a definite work in progress with zero talent for repairing old doors or leaky faucets.

Once the door was moving freely, Rhianna padded to the kitchen and tapped a paper on her counter. "You should go to this with me. It's next Tuesday evening."

A colorful flyer demanded his attention. *Reinvention Convention—Are You Struggling To Find Your Passion?*

He frowned. "Passion isn't exactly what I need at the moment. Besides, you know as well as I that we'd be sitting a room full of middle-aged women unhappy with their lives."

She sighed. "You don't know that."

Yes, he did. He hiked a brow in response.

She threw up her arms. "Okay, maybe there will be more women than men, but that's a *good* thing for a single, unattached man who—"

"Wants to stay single and unattached. Why does everyone in our family throw random women at me?"

Her eyes widened. "What are you talking about?"

"Mom took the liberty of hiring a decorator for my house."

She grinned, a dead giveaway she already knew. "Oh, really?"

He nodded. "Really, except *I* had to pay for it. There was a huge discount, but…she's trying to fix me up again." He wadded up the flyer on her counter and reached to toss it at the waste can.

"Hey." Rhianna grabbed for his hands. "I want that. I'm going with or without you."

"Oh, uh, my bad." He smoothed out the paper in a futile attempt to remove the creases. "Sorry, sis. I love you, but there's no way in hell I'm going to one of those rah-rah self-help things.

I'd rather pluck my whiskers out with a pair of pliers. That's a job for your husband. Your door's fixed. I'm going home. Have fun finding your passion." The only passion he had at the moment was for adventure. He didn't want any more busybody women steering his life. He seriously doubted her geek-a-zoid husband would oblige willingly either.

Roger shoved out the door before she had a chance to argue. At the office later, he dove into the paperwork and budgetary documentation for a project Carter and he were sharing. The sound of footsteps plodding on the carpet caught his attention. Someone else was working on a weekend?

"Knock, knock." Carter leaned in. "You shouldn't be here."

"You shouldn't either."

"I don't have a choice. By tomorrow morning, I'll be flying over the Atlantic."

"Need anything from me before you go?"

"Nah, just don't send any more of your fancy text messages about boobs, butts, or babes. Okay? I don't think Abby'd forgive me." Carter wasn't joking.

Carter had been commuting to Indonesia for months. No wonder he and Abby had had such a rocky start. It hadn't helped that Caroline pushed things along with erroneous text messages.

Which reminded him he hadn't looked at her blog in a few days. After Carter strode back to his office, Roger pulled up the browser link. He'd placed a shortcut on his desktop and fictitiously labeled it "News" just in case anyone looked.

Caroline was good with words. Funny, too. Her post today was about Love, Lust, and Lavender. A cute title. Apparently love is purple according to her blog post. He smiled as she rambled on about how much women love the scent of lavender.

Roger's eyes bugged at the last paragraph. "What the hell?"

For all you men who own big slobbering dogs that need discipline, the smell of dog fur and Purina isn't exactly the aphrodisiac a girl needs. Clean your place and burn a candle. If the animal is bent on marking his territory, buy a pot of lavender to mask him with something attractive in the scent category.

Was that a jab at him? Or maybe at Conan? He grunted. Scrolling down the screen, he read three comments that pissed him off further as women expounded on smelly dogs, underwear, gym clothes, and men's flatulence. *Hey, come on, women fart too. Besides, Conan doesn't stink. I wash him twice a week—more if he runs around in the dirt.* Surely he'd know if his place reeked of dog, right?

"I'll stick up for you, Conan." He was talking to thin air as he keyed in a response and pressed submit.

Chapter Seventeen

Two days later, Caroline recognized she had fallen into the role of marketing coordinator just as easily as Abby fell into the role of accountant and store manager. The creativity of marketing was similar to journalism, and being able to write from the heart was like fulfilling her destiny. Yes, corny but true. Maybe she was her father's daughter after all. It added a little bounce to her step as she waltzed to unlock the door, and she smiled at the cheerful jingle of their old-fashioned door alarm.

Abby and Carter were having breakfast together at the coffee shop down the street—a good descriptor for morning nookie. Thank God they'd finally had their come-to-Jesus meeting. It had taken months for them to sort out all their mistaken identities, which had grown exponentially more complicated with every text and online app. Geeze, those smart phones were dumb. She switched the sign to *Open* and skip-danced to the office in the back. She couldn't wait to write her next blog post about the epic adventures of her partner and the store.

The worst thing about having a business partner-slash-friend in a happy relationship? It made Caroline realize how perfectly and proportionately *un*happy her own life felt. Top that with being locked in the store with ex-flame and crazy-lech guy Roger for a few minutes of mind-numbing kissing, and Caroline wanted to barf. She still hadn't forgiven Abby for that gimmick. Abby said he'd begged for a few minutes alone with her to talk. But then he hadn't talked; he'd *criticized*.

Who the hell was he to tell her how much *she'd* changed? Had he traveled the world seeking a news media career comparable to her father's? Had he witnessed the inhumane cruelties of third-world countries and intolerable abuse of children and women?

No. He hadn't even left his fricking hometown. The smug, over-snarky prick. Speaking of changes, he'd turned into a marshmallow. Not fat, but soft and lacking in adventure. Ironic, considering he'd been the one with all the fancy big-ass plans of becoming an entrepreneur. How could he judge her for pursuing a personal dream of her own?

Crash. What the hell was that? The wheels of her chair squealed as she jolted up, spinning it across the small space. She rushed through the door.

"I'll pay for the damage. I promise." *Roger?* Caroline blinked to be sure.

"What are you doing?" Caroline hadn't seen him in a while and noted the way his jeans cuddled his body. They fit perfectly—dammit. Worn smooth in all the right places and slung low on his waist. His sockless feet were comfortably lodged into loafers, which bared a dapple of hair on the arches of his feet. She swallowed.

He bent to clean up the debris from the plant he'd knocked over. The guy was a walking, talking wrecking ball. He met her gaze. "I thought I'd sign up for one of those package deals you're advertising. You know, the one on your website."

She folded her arms and cocked a brow. "For a girl or guy?"

Roger stood and mirrored her gesture—showing his normal sass. Or should she say "ass"?

"A guy? Seriously? What guy wants flowers?"

She opened her mouth to speak, but he held up a finger to silence the words.

"Don't. It's for a girl—actually, a group of girls."

Caroline rolled her eyes and rounded the counter to get her enrollment book for the BFB service. "Of course."

"What the hell is that supposed to mean? I have sisters, okay?"

Caroline could probably get on board with selling flowers to a sister or two. "None of my business. We just need names and addresses for the recipients on this form." She slid a blank page his way. "Here's a pen."

He browsed the paper. "I'll need two of these."

"You're kidding, right?"

Roger shook his head, and she noted the scruffiness of beard growth at his cheeks. Was he growing it out, or had he just forgotten to shave? "Nope, three sisters plus my mother—but you already knew that. Or have you forgotten more than just our body heat?"

"Yeah, it's a shocker really. Who'd have guessed your charming ass was surrounded by a hoard of women based on your…" She let her voice trail off before she divulged the insult going through her mind.

"My what?"

Caroline shrugged. "Um, demeanor?"

Roger stared for a second. Was he going to blow up? She looked around. Abby was gone, so no one was around to back her up or protect her if he went ape-shit. He blinked—then grinned. "Good answer, Caro. Perfectly worded to puncture holes in my ego."

She shrugged and slipped another form his way. "I try."

"Do you?"

"What? You act like I don't. Like I'm…*trying* to be snippy."

He cocked his head and focused on the forms for a moment. "I didn't mean to infer that."

"Then what exactly *were* you inferring?"

He finished filling out the forms in silence before pushing them back across the counter. "Nothing, Caroline." A grumbling noise came from his torso. Caroline glanced at the time on her phone. Where was Abby? She should be back by now.

"You're hungry." Based on the noise emitted from his stomach, more like starving.

"Yeah, a little. It's lunchtime."

"You skipped eating to do this?" What a thoughtful brother.

He pulled a credit card from his wallet and tossed it on the counter. "Not exactly. I thought I'd drop in first then grab a bite on the way back—unless of course you're hungry."

Caroline swiped the card. "You're asking me out to lunch?"

Without meeting her gaze, he shoved the card back into his wallet. "You have to eat. I have to eat. We can do it together. Or not. Doesn't matter to me. Your choice."

She frowned. "Who's snippy now?" The door jingled and she turned to greet the newcomer. "Oh. Hi, Abby."

Abby entered with a box under her arm and a Cheshire grin on her face. Based on her expression, she'd had lunch *and* a quickie with Carter. She waved at Roger and strode to the office. She hadn't seemed at all surprised to see him.

Roger grinned. "Perfect timing. So, what's the verdict? Together? Or not?"

She hesitated. Together? Them? Never. She didn't care how long he stared at her with those melt-me chocolate eyes. *Stop. Oh boy, I'm in trouble.* "Um, okay."

Her assent took him by complete surprise. *Now what?* He hadn't thought that far ahead. He followed Caroline out the door fully aware they hadn't decided where to go or what to eat. Glancing up and down her petite frame, a smile crept across his lips at the wild colors in her shirt and leggings. They were almost as vibrant as the color she'd added to her eyelids. She turned and waited. "Do we have a destination, or are we just going to walk aimlessly along the street until something strikes our interest?"

Good question. One he didn't have an answer for. He shrugged. "Aimless wandering sounds good to me." He stuck his hands in his pockets and cocked his head toward the corner. "Come on."

She flicked her eyes at the clouds and shrugged. "Same guy, different environment."

"Of course. Leopards don't change their spots. But seriously, I have an idea." He pulled a hand from his pocket and flicked his fingers. "Let's motivate, gorgeous."

"Motivate?" She followed in short, quick steps.

"Yep. Motivated moving. There's a sub shop by the police station. We can get sandwiches and take them over to the park. It's such a pretty day that I'd rather spend the time outside, wouldn't you?"

"Sure." At the streetlight, they waited silently for the color to change. Caroline spotted a nearby billboard advertising an art function at the hospital.

"My mother was there."

He glanced sideways. "Come again?"

She pointed at the sign. "My mother was ill—she was in the hospital there."

He followed her fingers to the sign. *Oh.* "I know."

She jerked her eyes to his. "You do?"

What should he say? Now wasn't the time to mention he'd met the woman. "Yeah, I think Abby said something about her being sick after you graduated."

The light flicked green, and the people around them began walking. "Oh, well, yes. Actually she died not too long after I returned from that internship."

He knew that, too, but it wasn't the time for *that* discussion either. It might never be. "I'm sorry."

Caroline shrugged and focused on the billboard as they drew nearer. "She would have liked something like that. She took photography lessons for a few months. There's all sorts of pictures around the house and my dad's place that were hers."

Feigning newfound interest, he smiled. "Something to remember her by."

"Yeah." Caroline kept walking in silence. Unsure what to say next, he followed after taking one last glance at the sign.

"Wanna talk about it?"

The wind blasted them. He watched her chest rise and fall as she sucked in a deep breath. "No."

Once they reached the sub place, he pulled the door open for her. "Do you like mushrooms?"

Her eyebrows hitched in a very cute and confused tilt. He glanced at her mouth.

"What?"

"Mushrooms. They make a sandwich here called the Tension Killer. It has four different kinds of meat, all sorts of vegetables, and fried mushrooms with a layer of cream cheese."

Her mouth tilted as if squelching a smile as she surveyed the menu. "Really?"

"I swear."

When she lifted her eyes to his, it was all he could do to keep from bending down to take that mouth. She looked amazing, in a crazy, sad, and vulnerable way. "Oh, I see it. Is it good?"

Roger shrugged. He had no idea. "I've never had the courage to try it. It sounds dangerous."

Caroline shifted from one foot to the other and lifted her lips in a devilish dare. "I will if you will. Let's share one."

He laughed. "How did I know you'd say that?"

She blinked her eyes in an innocently sexy way. "Like you said, leopards don't change their spots." She punched an index finger to his chest then back at herself. "You sane, me crazy."

She had that backwards, but he'd let her learn on her own how un-sane he really was. He gave their order to the guy at the counter.

Chapter Eighteen

"Who's Caro?" Ruth Freeman didn't bother with small talk once a bee had gotten under the family blanket. It was a pretty damn crowded blanket with Roger and his three siblings, but somehow she always had a keen sense of what belonged and didn't.

"What?"

Why'd he agree to grill for them? She tapped the yellow pad on his coffee table. "Caro." Oooh. He really should find another outlet for his idleness other than doodling. His drawings were almost like a diary, and people always wanted to analyze the results.

"No one," he lied.

"Then why does it have a hammer there pounding on your brain? Or is that someone else's brain?" His mother squinted. "It looks like a stomach, complete with a pile of intestines."

"Mom."

"A psychiatrist would say that's a clear sign someone is driving you crazy…someone named Caro or—"

"It's Caroline. And she's not driving me crazy. She *is* crazy."

"Why do you say that?"

He should've kept his mouth shut, but Caroline's blog continued to rant about men in general, and for some reason he'd taken it personally. His morning routine included a steady roll of responses perfectly worded to defend the male species. Of course he'd kept his identity secret. His blog name was totally original, something she'd never guess. Frederick, in honor of his hound. He'd named Conan after a guy named Frederick Conan, one of his neighbors in college. For some reason, Roger thought he looked a lot like his new puppy, though he'd never confessed as much.

"She used to be so different. She was fun and smart and talented and—"

His mother focused on his face, causing him to squirm. "Used to be? How long have you known this woman, and why haven't I heard anything about her? Wait." She took a step forward and planted a hand on his forearm. "Is this that girl from college? The one you wanted us to meet?"

"That's the one."

She squeezed his arm. "So she's back?"

He turned to pick up his iPad, faking boredom as he rattled his head. "Nope. Not in that sense. She's back in town, though, runs a florist shop downtown. Here's their blog." He thrust the screen toward his mother.

"Oh. That's nice. So, you're still seeing Marina then? I like Marina. She's perfect for you."

He snickered. "She's perfect for *you*, you mean. No, I'm not seeing Marina. We've had dinner or lunch a couple of times, that's all."

His mother scrolled a finger across his tablet. He tried to move away, but she reached a hand out and pulled it from his grasp, surveying the screen. "They have some nice stuff. I'll have to go by and check it out sometime."

He stiffened. Oh, hell no. "You mean check *her* out, don't you?"

"Of course not. I just…you never know when you might need a nice gift or a trinket for a party."

He sighed. "Riiiiight."

"Don't be ugly now. Besides, whatever happened to the college girl? One minute you couldn't wait for us to meet her, and the next she was on the other side of the world."

Rebecca lifted her head from the textbook she'd buried herself into, "Yep, she sure couldn't wait to ditch your ass."

"Hey, watch it." Roger frowned as Conan took the cue and growled. Unfortunately, his wagging tail made him appear less than threatening.

"Face it, brother. You suck with women. No wonder Mom had to find you a girlfriend."

"She's not—and we're not dating."

"Then why was she leaving your place at one a.m. on a Friday?"

His mother switched her focus from the tablet to Rebecca. "Which one? Marina or Caro…line?"

Rebecca shrugged. "I don't know. Tall, sleek, wild blonde hair."

Ruth nodded and smiled. "Marina."

Rebecca gasped. "Then who's Caroline?"

Roger sighed. "None of your business. You're spying on me now, sis?"

Rebecca shuttled a glance at their mother, then shrugged. "I went out with some friends, but they didn't want to take me home. I was gonna crash here until I saw some chick in the window. When I called Mom—"

"You called Mom to tell her there was a woman in my apartment? Seriously?"

Ruth patted his head. "Relax. She was just looking out for you."

"Was she now? Sounds to me like her nose was bent from sticking it in my business."

Rebecca patted Conan and tapped her pen on the table. The stiletto noise clicked through the silence. "I was debating whether to call you and ask if I could stay when she walked out the door."

"You saw us?"

At least Rebecca had the decency to blush—and keep tapping the damn pen. "Yeah. Nice set of tonsils. I wasn't sure if she was coming out or going back in for a quickie. Or maybe you already…"

Roger held up a hand. That was none of their business. "Stop."

Ruth darted a glance between her kids. "So, you're still seeing her. Why the note about Caro, or Caroline? You aren't playing both sides of the card, are you?"

Roger yanked the pen from Rebecca's hand. "I said stop. I'm not playing any cards. I'm not dating either one of them. And I don't need you guys spying on poor girls at work in order to find me a date. I can get one on my own."

Ruth grinned. "Great! Then bring one of them to dinner this weekend." Her cell beeped. "Oh, I have a message." She dug through her bag, pulled out the device, then glanced at the screen. "I'd better go."

Relief flooded Roger's shoulders. "Someone needs you?"

She frowned. "Not really. Odd. Someone *remembers* me. Not sure who this is. His name is Landon. The only Landon I know was from years ago, and I haven't—" Her cell beeped again. "Oh. Ummm, look, I'll see you guys this weekend. Bring that date, Roger." She pointed a finger in warning before tossing her cell in her purse and rushing out.

His mother was texting? Weird. "That was strange." He watched the door as it slammed closed.

Rebecca nodded. "No kidding. You think she knows she forgot me?"

The door flung open, and Ruth's hair fell over flushed cheeks. "You coming or not?"

Roger swallowed a grin and nodded at his baby sister. "Asked and answered."

After the car's engine roared away, he picked up his cell and called Caroline. It rang three times before she answered. "You busy this weekend?" he asked.

"Yes."

Okay that was a stupid idea. Why'd he try?

He heard a popping noise. "I'm working. We take turns doing the weekend shift, and I have this one. Why?" More popping.

"What's that noise?"

A couple seconds ticked by. "Oops. I like to pop those little air bubbles they pack the plants in. I'm addicted to it. Can't help myself."

He smiled. "My mother read your blog."

"Really? Why?"

He searched for an appropriate response. Probably shouldn't tell her he'd been doodling about her and calling her crazy. He had no intention of admitting to commenting regularly on her blog either. "I don't know. I guess she saw one of your ads in the paper." Before she could ask anything else, he forged further. "It's a great blog. I suppose someone with your journalistic background finds it easy to write all that stuff."

"Not really, but we're struggling. The *store* is struggling. If I keep writing, people keep reading. Sometimes it gets them in the store out of curiosity. The business is improving as a result. I've also accumulated a few weirdos along the way, but I guess that goes with the territory."

"Weirdos?"

"Yeah, some ass-wipe blogger keeps leaving snarky comments. People seem to like him though."

He feigned ignorance. "That's good. So, the weekend's out—what about tonight?" He sucked in his gum and coughed. His eyes watered. Had he really asked *again*? "Never mind, I was just kid—"

"Sure."

She said yes? "Oh. Great. You can fill me in on your trek across Europe and how the contract reporter thing went."

Silence fell between them like a cannonball.

He tried to recover. "Or we could just, you know, talk about the shop. Or me. That's always a good subject."

He heard a snicker. At least she found him funny. "Sounds *fabulous*. That should take, what, a minute or two? You're such an interesting guy, you know."

"Ouch. Nice. Worst-case scenario, we eat and listen to the music or the conversations around us. How much time do you need to get ready?"

Pop. Pop. Pop. The bubbles were taking a beating again. Was she nervous or bored? "I'm at work and can't leave until I close up at eight."

"I'll be there at eight."

• • •

At seven thirty, the door jangled open, and Caroline was mildly annoyed to see Roger approach. She had wanted to comb her hair and put a touch of makeup on, but the shop had been busy. "You said eight."

"I thought you might want some help, and I was bored."

"I can handle this. I just have to unbox some stock and lock up. *You* are a distraction."

"What? You can't handle me *and* this?" He gestured at the shop.

She arched a brow. "Are you baiting me to say something stupid so you can deliver a clever comeback like 'I'll let you handle me any time'? Or maybe 'wanna lock me up too'? Or—"

Roger plucked a leaf from a plant. She gave him her best chastising glare. He returned a dimpled grin. "I can do those things. Or I can leave. Your choice."

She wanted to slap his rude face, but instead she pulled a box knife from the drawer and pointed it toward him. "You can stay. But I know how to use this, so behave yourself."

"When have I not behaved?"

Her insides did a little somersault at the thought as she took a trip to the past and relived a memory or two. That was the thing. She wasn't really interested in going back there—but she sure liked remembering.

"I don't think I want to answer that question."

Roger held up his hands in surrender then slowly turned a palm over and flicked his fingers in request. "I'll do the boxes. Where are they?"

She held her back stiff as he followed her to the stockroom. She showed him what to do and returned to the store. A few minutes later, a laugh bellowed from the depths of the room.

"What's so funny?" she called, not wanting to go see. She didn't trust herself in that small room with him. Not for long.

"Your partner's screensaver. When did you guys take these pictures?" His voice echoed through the door.

Uh-oh. Damn, she wished she'd thought about the computer before letting him into their private space. A chill settled in her shoulders. It was one thing for Abby to make a video of their skinny-dipping experience in the freezing cold water in France. It was something totally different to have a complete stranger view her bare ass as she tiptoed to the edge and did a screaming belly-flop into the murky water. Over and over. Abby had thought it hilarious to edit the clip so that it could be viewed on a loop.

Okay, he wasn't a total stranger. He was Roger. Her old flame from college. Correction: old friend. No, that wasn't right either. Hell, she didn't really know *what* he was. Except here in her stockroom, laughing at naked pictures of *her*. She checked the time. Ten minutes to closing. "Oh, hell, no one's going to come in this late."

She twisted the lock into place, flipped the lights off, and stomped to the back. The door clanked against a shelf as she flung it open. "Stop looking at—" She stopped mid-sentence.

Roger had emptied the boxes, placed the contents as directed, and folded the cardboard and stowed it near their back door. At the moment, he was reclined in the office chair with one leg flung up on the desk as he rocked back and forth. The chair creaked under his weight, and he dropped his feet. A daisy stem dangled from his teeth like a cigar. He pulled it from his lips and pointed at the screen with the flower. "These are amazing. Was Abby with you over there? I don't remember her from school."

Of course he didn't. "We met in France and traveled together for a while, then went our separate ways when I had to report on an upheaval in the Middle East. It was my big chance."

He nodded. "Everyone needs one of those. How'd that turn out for ya?"

Not worth a shit, but she'd never admit as much. She shrugged, thankful that her hands weren't shaking. That subject was off-limits no matter how many times he asked. "It wasn't as big a deal as I'd hoped."

He frowned. "Or maybe it was bigger."

She tossed her head back and dropped a hand to her hip. "What does that mean?"

The chair squeaked as he rose to tower above her. He leaned in and whispered, "It means I read about you a lot over the last few days. There's a lot more to that story than you want to admit, beautiful."

A knot formed in her stomach. "There's nothing to read. It was a bust. I didn't write the piece because I messed up. That's why I came home: I stunk at finding and reporting the story. Someone else got the job a week later." There were approximately two inches between his mouth and hers. Two inches of cold, steel-hardened air. She glanced at his mouth. She could close that gap in a second if she could move. But she couldn't. What would he do? She blinked.

His breath feathered against her face. "The story's there. It's still in your head. I can see it in your eyes. Whatever happened over there branded you, sweetness." He tapped a finger to her forehead to signal the imprint.

Caroline took a step backward. She forced the shudder from her shoulders. "Don't call me that. Let's get out of here."

"No, let's see the rest of your pictures from Europe. Show me." He tapped a finger to a key. The screensaver disappeared, replaced by a password prompt.

Gulp. She was *not* showing him those. TMI. Too personal. Too…everything. She shrugged innocently. "I don't know Abby's password."

"Really? I doubt your partner has any secrets."

Dang. He was right, had read her like a book in fact, a trait she hated about him. Abby shared everything with her; after all, they *were* partners. Of course there was the fact that Abby had misled his friend Carter for months through texting and secret identities. She hoisted a brow. "You're kidding, right? Abby?"

"Good point. Okay, I won't force you to show something that makes you uncomfortable. You hungry? What do you feel like, sushi?" His hand enclosed hers with warmth as he pulled her from the room.

She felt her body depressurize as she followed him from the store and down the street. Now she just needed to clamp the lid shut on any more questions about Europe.

His cell beeped. Caroline noted he shot it a glance then returned it to darkness. "Please don't tell me you're a text-o-holic like your buddy Carter. I'd rather stick pins in my eyeballs than share a meal with social media.."

He hefted his shoulders up and down. "Strange metaphor. Don't worry. Carter is overseas at the moment, and I have a conference call with him later. Just wanted to make sure we were still on because if he canceled, I'd have all the time in the world tonight. If not, I'd have to work in a few hours."

"Oh. Okay."

"Nice ass, by the way." She remembered how Roger had smiled at the image of two bikini-less girls on the computer before they left.

She punched his arm.

Chapter Nineteen

Roger turned his Land Rover into the parking lot of the museum. Caroline swiveled to survey a set of neon signs announcing that the museum was hosting a fundraiser. "They serve sushi here?"

He shook his head. "I promised a friend I'd stop in if her pictures were ever chosen for display."

Caroline frowned. "You're taking me to a fundraiser? Why didn't you say something? I'm not dressed for—"

He reached out and grabbed her hand as the engine died. "You look great. We'll only be here a minute or two. I have to stop in and say hello to the people who coordinated this, and then we can go. Besides, you're a photographer. This is right up your alley."

He grabbed his collar and pulled. It was a stupid idea to attend, and she'd probably go ape-shit when she saw the pictures. Still, he had to at least make an appearance. He'd planned to take her over the weekend, which would have given him a chance to prepare her for the shock. But he wasn't about to give up an opportunity to get her out for an evening alone. That kiss had fueled his imagination for a short while, but it wasn't enough.

He stepped from the vehicle and walked to open her door. With it open and waiting, he figured she had two choices. One, sit there while he went in. Two, get out and join him. Of course, there *was* a third option that involved hailing a cab, but she wasn't that rude.

The foggy evening cast a surreal haze over the glowing neon inside the windows. Silhouettes of people entering the building beckoned them to follow.

"This is a fundraiser? What for?"

He hesitated for a second. Hopefully she wouldn't freak this soon. "The oncology ward at St. Jude's."

She stilled to a statuesque pose. Her face went ashen. "Nuh-uh. I hate hospitals. My mother—"

He grabbed her arm. "I know. Your mother was ill. Don't worry, we're not going to the hospital, and there aren't any patients here as far as I know. Just a lot of artwork. It's even a silent auction, so it'll be all the more...quiet."

He clutched her arm until they'd weaved through the crowded entrance and past the greeters. How he'd managed to slip by without being stopped was a feat in itself. "Roger," a voice called.

Damn, wishful thinking.

He turned around, expecting the art exhibit's coordinator. Instead...

"Dad?" Caroline's eyes popped. She pivoted her eyes between the two men. "You guys know each other?"

Roger cleared his throat. How should he continue?

Her father pasted on a smile that indicated a shared secret between the two. "Of course we do. He was here when I delivered our donation for the event. Have you seen Carol's picture? They hung it down at the end. She would have been so glad. The bids are already over a thousand. I can't believe it."

Yikes. That wasn't exactly how Roger planned to break the news.

Caroline squinted toward the darkened hall. "Wait. What? Mom's picture? What are you talking about?" She clip-clopped away in search of it.

He had planned to do this gradually. Show her all the other photos. The ones of the beach. Of the kids. Of Conan. Then, when she'd adjusted to them, and if she was in a decent mood, he'd show her Carol. He'd hoped it would melt her heart to see how beautiful the picture had turned out.

"She doesn't know, does she?" His father's solemn voice was like lead.

Roger shook his head. "I only submitted them a couple of days ago on a whim. It seemed like a good tribute, and I never had a chance to—"

Bob cursed and sped after his daughter. "I'll be back to find out why the hell you brought my daughter here. Idiot." An elderly gentleman who had accompanied Bob trailed after him at a snail's space. He repeated the curse as he worked his ancient legs in an effort to follow.

"Because she deserves to know," Roger muttered to thin air.

What should he do? Cut her off in the hallway? He should have skipped the event, but he'd promised to attend.

"Is that my foot?" a voice shrieked. Damn. Roger felt his face flush. She'd seen the first picture. "And my…backside? Are you *kidding* me?" Damn.

Crash. A picture on an easel dipped and tumbled. Roger rushed over and tried to catch it but missed. Two others hit the floor as Caroline thrashed and cursed. Her cheeks flamed to match the red ribbon she'd tied at her neck. She held up a finger and crooked it. Straight. At him.

"You."

He looked around. "Who?"

"You know who. You took these?"

"Uh." He wasn't sure—had he? His brain went blank. "Uh."

"You can't *do* that. You can't take pictures of people and plaster them all over the damn place without permission. You can't…"

Her arms were spinning like a windmill. If she kept going, she would twist out of her sockets.

"Caroline. Calm down." Her father arrived and pulled her into a bear hug. "You're making a scene."

She sputtered. "Scene? This guy takes pictures of me years ago and then blows them up and displays them here for, for—"

"A good cause. It's for a good cause, honey. Besides, until you blurted the newsflash, there wasn't any way to know these were of you. Your face isn't on a single one."

"No, just my ass." She pointed at one of the spilled frames. "And my leg. And—oh crap, is that my…Jesus Christ." She attempted to bend and look at the picture below, but her father held her tight.

The elderly gentleman finally bulldozed behind Caroline's father, holding his arms out wide. He flung them around the man and his daughter and grinned. Had he called out *bear hug*? He grunted something else before the three toppled over, taking another easel with them.

Caroline shoved the two men off and crawled out from under a framed picture. She held up a thin forefinger. "Roger Freeman, get me the hell out of here before I explode in your face."

He glanced around. Hmmm. Judging by the state of the room, it was too late. Did that mean the sushi was canceled, too? His stomach growled in protest.

She lifted to one knee then stood erect. "Never mind. I'll find my own way out."

Don Carlisle, the organizer of the event, whispered into Roger's ear. "It sucks to be you, man. I was wondering…does this mean those pieces are no longer available? I need to know because there were bids on them. We need every penny."

Roger held up a hand and stuttered. "Hold that thought." He ran after Caroline, silently thanking her for wearing crazy colors instead of a fancy dress. It made her easy to spot—until she bolted into the women's room.

He waited. And waited. The door swished open. Two random women exited. No Caroline. How long would she hide out in there?

Minutes ticked by. She had to come out eventually; there were no other exits. Her father swung by and handed him a glass of scotch and soda. "This'll calm her a little."

Roger took one look at the liquid and tossed it back in three gulps. Forget her, he needed a little calming himself. He hadn't really thought the whole thing through. He thought she'd, just maybe, like the pictures? Dumb.

He knocked on the bathroom door. No answer. He knocked again. "Caro. You have to come out sometime."

"Go away."

"Why? They're just photos. They don't even show anything."

"Like hell they don't." Okay, maybe the one showed the shadow of her ass, but until she'd screamed no one could tell. Across the room, a crowd had gathered by the pictures and started to point. Shit, they were figuring it out now. Or at least trying to. So much for abstract art.

That was what Carlisle had called them. He liked the colors. Hell, Roger figured it was for a good cause, and he'd stared at them long enough. In snapshot form, of course, not quite as big as they were now.

A man walked his wife to the door and stood waiting as she went in. "Can you believe the one picture is at ten thousand dollars? Isn't that crazy?"

Roger's throat went dry. "Seriously? Which one?"

"I don't know. It has red and tan and—"

"Green. It has green in it." Caroline's voice wavered as she held the bathroom door open. "There was a green string to the suit, and it was barely tied and coming undone."

Actually, it had come completely undone and was lying on the towel in little ringlets, but who wanted to argue? The man's eyes darted from Caroline to Roger.

Roger played it safe and shrugged. "I don't know what she's talking about." It was a good idea to play dumb at the moment.

"Are you serious about the ten-thousand-dollar bid?" Caroline's voice held more than a hint of disbelief.

The man nodded. Roger kept silent. He wasn't sure what to do. When her eyes locked on his, her anger had dampened somewhat. "You should have told me."

Yes, he should have. He would have, too, if he hadn't been a complete idiot and thought she'd find it cute. He nodded, unable to respond.

Caroline ran a hand down her shirt and straightened the hem. "Who was that old guy who tackled me?"

He shrugged. "I don't know. He came with Bob. You want to stay or go? Or maybe beat me into a bag of crumbs?"

She thought for a second. "Hmmm, the bag of crumbs sounds good." She headed for the side exit near the bathroom. "Let me think about it for a while."

He had no choice but to follow as she pushed out into the night air and headed toward his car. Hmmm, she had something on her back. He squinted. The sauce from one of the snacks the wait staff handed out. Yuck. Should he tell her? He was reaching into his pocket for the napkin when she whirled around.

"You know what I don't understand? Where did you get those pictures? We went to the beach one time. Period. And you didn't have a camera. I took mine, but I don't recall—"

"You were sleeping, remember? You lathered up with lotion and dozed off on your towel."

"Okay, but—"

"You'd untied that string on your back to avoid tan lines, and I, um, got your camera out and snapped a couple of shots. There's one of you drooling on the towel—be glad I didn't share *that*."

She frowned. "Small victories. Which one is better for the art museum: me drooling on a towel or baring my backside? You obviously took more than just a couple shots." She felt violated.

"Your backside wasn't bare. Don't be ridiculous. It was just a close-up of the tie on the towel and the shadow of your hipbone. You had sand on your skin, and it—"

"Sparkled, yeah, I saw that. I should complain. Or sue." She yanked open the passenger door of the Land Rover and slid into the car, slamming the door.

• • •

He hadn't even asked. She could tell the pictures were of her from the tiny flower tattoo on her foot. Otherwise, the pictures were anonymous and random.

"Caro, I wasn't planning—"

"What? To share skin pictures of me? Or to get caught? Why'd you take me to see all this then? What was so important about showing me your, your voyeurism fetish?"

His eyes widened. "Voyeurism? It was just a close-up of a piece of string, a towel, and an inch or two of skin. How do you figure that as voyeuristic?"

"You watched me."

"Yes."

"You took pictures."

"Yes, with your camera. Not from far away. I was right there next to you."

She snapped her seatbelt into place. "If you took them with my camera, why don't I have the images? Why didn't I—"

"I kept the sim card. I pulled it and put in a new one. I thought you might get upset."

Her lip curled into a grimace. "Well you got that right."

They rode in silence to the restaurant. She debated asking him to take her home, but her stomach had passed the growling stage. It barked.

Not to mention, she was curious what else was on that sim card.

They ordered and ate the first few bites in silence. Outside, rain began to slap the window. She pointed her chopsticks at his nose. "You realize what's going to happen now?"

He stuffed a piece of peppered tuna in his mouth and chewed. When he'd swallowed the bite, he pinched another. "What's that?"

"If those really sell for that much, every guy there is going to ask you to take pictures of his wife or girlfriend. You'll be inundated with—"

"Naked women modeling for me? Sweet, I hadn't thought of it that way." He grinned. Caroline wanted to reach over and shove his face in the soy sauce. "The terrible price of fame. I could sell the pictures and make a mint."

"Yeah, you wish. Don't get a big head. It's a charity event, not the Smithsonian."

"Don't burst my bubble."

"I can see it now." She raised a hand and waved it across a fictitious billboard. "Freeman's Photo Fantasies. Your girl in all her glory."

"Hmmm. Catchy." He took a sip of rice wine.

"Should work real well for you, knowing how much you enjoy surveying women's curves."

His eyes narrowed over his glass as he drew in another sip. Was he searching for a response? He spotted something over Caroline's shoulder. Or someone. "Shit." He plunked the wine glass on the tablecloth.

"Roger! I'm glad you're here. I was planning to stop by later tonight."

Caroline looked up, then leaned back to get the full view and height of the woman who towered over their table in six-inch heels. Blonde waves cascaded over the shoulders of a perfectly fitted silk blouse, which fell smoothly over a rather *tight* skirt.

"Marina, I'm a little busy right now. Can we talk some other time?"

"I can stop by later, if you like…" The woman slid into the seat beside Roger.

"No! Don't stop by. Don't sit. Don't—"

Marina glanced at Caroline and blinked. "Oh, you're working."

Roger's hair fell in his eyes as he hitched it to the side. How long had the man gone without a haircut? "Nope, not working. Marina, this is Caroline. Caroline, Marina." He waved to acknowledge both women.

That was an introduction? No explanation, just names? Could this be one of his bevy of sisters? Caroline scrutinized her features. No, not in this lifetime. The only way she'd be a sibling was if she'd been adopted. Not to mention the panic—or was it guilt?—written all over his features.

Caroline had witnessed scenes like this on television but never in person—when the guy runs into two of his exes at once. Or maybe only one ex—her—and one current woman of the moment? Hmmm. Funny.

The warm buzz of the rice wine debated. Caroline dropped both palms to the table and rose. "Well, I can see you two need to talk. I'll just make a trip to the ladies' room then take off. Thanks!" She waggled her fingers and tromped away.

Now what?

Chapter Twenty

Caroline stared at her reflection in the mirror. The spiked, short hair was getting old. Time for a change. She changed hairstyles almost as much as that blonde girl probably changed shoes. So what? She liked the variety. Besides, she still had no idea who the woman staring back at her, through all the wild colors and hair, really was. She kept searching for meaning, but none ever came.

What was she doing hiding out in bathrooms to avoid Roger and the calamities that followed him? Wasn't that indication enough that she should keep away? She scrolled through her text messages. One from her father caught her eye.

Did you know your toes are worth more than my car?

She grinned. Okay, the pictures weren't exactly vulgar or indecent. A bit provocative maybe, but not completely nasty. She smiled at herself. Very provocative, actually. She wished that kind of artistic blood flowed through her veins. "It's for a good cause," she told her reflection.

A toilet flushed and a fiftyish well-dressed woman with dyed blonde hair stepped to the mirror. She pulled a lipstick out and leaned forward. "Honey, they're all a charity case at some point."

Caroline frowned. "Who?"

The woman waved the lipstick. "Men. I assumed that was what you were talking about. Was I wrong? Sometimes we need them desperately and other times they need us. Yin and yang. Give and get. It's what makes everything work."

Caroline's current mood didn't condone correcting the woman's impression. She wasn't making over Roger, and she certainly didn't *need* him—or his numerous issues. Nor did he need her. "Good point. Thanks." She exited the bathroom and weaved her way around the corner of the room, conveniently avoiding the table she'd vacated earlier.

What a stellar evening. Roger sure knew how to entertain. She shoved through the door of the restaurant, relieved that she hadn't been called. A gust of wind roared into her face. Now, if she could just find a ride home without having to deal with—

"Hi." Roger's vehicle idled on the curb of the restaurant. Front and center with him leaned against it. A toothpick dangled from his mouth. "Thought I'd just wait for you here, considering how long you take in the ladies' room."

Caroline growled. "Where's Mandy or Marny or whatever her name is?"

He shrugged. "Marina. Don't know. I left her at the table after the check was paid. You ready?"

If there was a cab in sight, she'd have taken it—but there wasn't. She stepped to the vehicle, and he opened the door. "Yeah."

"Good. Did you know your feet are worth a small fortune? I got a call from Don a minute ago. That picture of your toes trailing in the sand sold for seven grand, and the one with green that you liked topped out a little over eleven."

She hadn't said she *liked* it; she'd just recognized everything *in* it.

He rounded the vehicle and joined her. When the car revved into action, she grunted. "Just shows you how stupid people can become when it's for a good cause."

"Or generous. You won't believe what that little shot of your hip went for."

She rolled her eyes. "I don't want to know."

He snickered. "Too funny."

"Pictures of body parts on sand aren't exactly art, you know. People take those all the time. In fact, I took some…" Shit. Just like that, her thoughts went across the world to a tiny body rattled with gunshot. Sprawled in pieces on sand like a fine steak displayed on dirty rice.

Seconds dragged into minutes as he waited for her to finish, but it wasn't possible for her to continue. When he pulled into the drive at her house, she hopped out and headed for the door. One. Two. Three. Four steps. Six more, and she'd—

A steel grip clamped around her wrist and whirled her backward. Right into his chest. Polo cologne blasted her senses as his warm fingers took her by the chin and lifted until their gaze met. Was that sympathy in those big brown babies? No. She didn't want it—didn't need to be coddled. The creases of the dimples caught in her porch light, but his mouth never arched at the sides. "Go ahead. Finish what you were saying, Caro. Tell me."

She jutted her chin. "I was just going to say I took some, too. They just weren't as good. That's all. You should think about changing colognes, or cars, or shoe styles. You haven't changed at all in six years. You even smell the same. Change is good, right?" He *had* changed. She lied because she desperately needed to get into her house and close the door. He'd changed from a sweet-faced boy into a devilish-dimpled—whoa.

Roger crushed her mouth with his. No warning. Nothing. A nice, warm kiss that lasted longer than she'd expected—a kiss that slipped into something much, much more. Before she knew what was happening, his tongue was stroking hers, and her malfunctioning brain cells decided not to intervene. Instead they must have left her head completely, because she pulled him inside the door and onto the couch.

All she could see in the light filtering through her living-room window shade were—dimples. Damn it all to hell, she loved his dimples. She moved her mouth down to drop a little action into the left one, just a slight kiss, then he slid out from under her and she fell. Flat on her ass onto the carpet. "What's wrong?"

He sat on the couch panting and shook his head. His hair flopped from side to side. No words. Was he speechless?

"Why'd you stop?"

More panting. He swallowed. "You're like a yo-yo: up one minute, mad as hell the next. Then this—wow. You scare the shit out of me, Caro." He chuckled between breaths.

She smiled. "Likewise." She leaned back on her elbows and slid her knee against him.

"And just for the record, I wasn't stopping. I just needed some space to breathe. I'd kind of forgotten this part."

What part? He'd forgotten how they were? "Forgotten? Was I that boring?" In truth, she'd never really dated anyone before him, so if he said yes, it wouldn't have surprised her. She had gone through a slew of men since.

His voice came low and husky as he crawled over her, his body stretched above hers arched and threatening. "No, no, not boring. Not even close. All-consuming, maybe."

She trailed a finger along the stubble on his chin. Yes, she'd always been prone to confrontation and pushing past her limits. Until now. "You say that like it's a bad thing."

"That's the part that terrifies me: I'm not sure if it is or isn't."

Funny thing was, she felt the same way about their odd chemistry. She frowned. One of the things about Roger she'd always *liked* was that he wasn't one of the dangerous types—the ones who chew women up and spit them out like splintered toothpicks. She'd encountered plenty of those. Sure, he *pretended* to be, but she wasn't born yesterday. Any man who had three sisters and still talked to them can't get away with much. Not when it comes to treating women badly. He was as in-your-face as she was, but when the rubber hit the road, he had a person's back. He expected the same, too, which posed a problem because she wasn't at all reliable. Not anymore, and *that* was the terrifying part.

She pushed him off and sat up. "You're right. We should stop."

No. Wait.

"Stop?" he said. "That wasn't what I meant."

She swallowed, trying to soothe the scratchiness in her voice. Why did it suddenly feel like a furnace was blasting her intestines? Unsure how to handle the situation, she chose to do what she did best—bark. "Back off, Roger."

Chapter Twenty-One

Caroline was clearing counters when Abby blasted through the door, bringing a wind in her wake that sent ribbons, leaves, and foil paper flying toward the ceiling. A Hail Mary to the forcefulness of her entry.

"I think I want to kiss you." Abby strode toward Caroline with arms wide, and Caroline half-expected her to actually plant a big wet one.

Jutting a hand up with fingers splayed, she grimaced. "Save it for that threesome Carter keeps talking about."

"We're over the hump."

"Ookkaaay. Glad to hear you guys are keeping it spicy." Or not—she really didn't want to hear the details. As much as she loved her friend, some things just needed to stay private.

Abby laughed and leaned over to pick up a few pieces of ribbon and confetti. She tossed them at Caroline. "Not *that* hump. The financial hump. We, as in you and your massively fantastic advertisements, have managed to get our store out of the bind we were in. We're having a black month."

"Black month? Don't you think that will come back to bite us?" She teased, knowing full well her implication.

"Yeah, funny. We need to celebrate. We should go out and have a girls' night. I can't believe we don't have to go to the bank for money this month. This is awesome, *you* are awesome, and I love you." Abby jumped on the counter and wrapped her arms around Caroline, drawing her in for a tight squeeze.

Caroline's throat tightened. "Awwg. Stop! You're choking me—and choking me up at the same time." She patted one of the arms that had lodged against her throat twice before slipping from the hug. "Girls' night sounds good. I could go for that. God knows we could both use a little relief."

That night they locked up and waltzed down the street to the bar across from the police station, an irony that Abby never hesitated to point out to anyone that would listen. Any idiot who walked out drunk and got into a car with the police across the street deserved a DUI. Yet, to her confusion, they'd never heard of even one occurrence. Of course, on any given day, there were three or more off-duty cops saddled against the bar with a frothy beer in their hand. Who would dare argue?

Caroline was deep into a vent about her blog-buddy, Frederick, when a waft of Polo caught her attention. She rotated and peered over a shoulder. *Crap.* "Did you tell Carter where we were?" Trailing behind Carter, with hands in pockets, was the very man she'd practically attacked on her living-room floor. She furrowed her eyebrows at Roger and glared at Abby, who simply shrugged.

"Yeah, that's okay, isn't it? He dropped me off this morning, and I needed a ride home." Abby hadn't mentioned which home—hers or Carter's. They'd recently become engaged in a very romantic fiasco at the Astros stadium. As much as Caroline hated to admit it, she'd almost shed a tear for their happiness.

"Do I have a say? I thought this was a *girls'* night out. They don't exactly fit the description."

"I know, I know. But sometimes you just have to be flexible. Carter's leaving tomorrow to go back overseas for two weeks for work. We have to—"

Caroline held up a hand. "Don't tell me. I get the picture."

Carter leaned over and dropped a big one on Abby's mouth. "You ready, babe?"

Caroline's ears registered the words. "Wait. You're leaving?"

Carter remained standing, while his accomplice, Roger, made use of the empty space beside Caroline. She probably should have scooted over and given him room, but—what the hell. She sighed and inched away from the warmth of an arm against her rib cage. *Fine, take the seat if you want it.*

Abby rose and nodded while taking the last sip of her beer. "Yeah, sorry. We're making Chinese tonight. You ever tried making shrimp wontons? They're fun." She giggled and glanced at Carter in way that suggested some sort of inside joke.

They left. Caroline blinked as the door whooshed shut, leaving her alone with Roger and his massive dimples. The last time she'd seen them—him—she was up close to those babies and trying to taste them.

Awkward.

"Well, here we are." She focused on her beer glass, inwardly cursing herself for the last order of Corona the barmaid placed in front of her.

Roger held up two fingers. The girl nodded and was gone.

She didn't dare touch her drink. "I just want you to know the only reason I'm not making a big deal about those pictures— which you've shared with the entire world—is because of how much money you raised for the hospital."

He turned his gaze to meet hers. "Okay."

"Plus no one can actually tell it was me, and they *were* good. I never knew you liked photography."

"You inspired me."

She rolled her eyes.

Roger ran a finger along the rim of his glass. "I'm serious. I remembered all the pictures you took and the excitement you had for that trip. It all sounded so glamorous. I wished…" His voice trailed to silence.

She swallowed a tiny lump. "Yeah, well, look how it all ended. I bombed, and here I am now, pursuing—whatever."

"You own a business."

"A flower business. Did you ever think I'd be into plants?"

He shrugged. "Actually, I'm not surprised at all. You were always growing something on your porch, so for you to make it a part of your income is great. I just thought your heart was set on journalism."

She sighed. "People change."

"Not always."

He was right. He hadn't. She admired that now. "True. You, Rog, have stayed on task and kept your promises. Rock solid, that's you."

He groaned. "You make me sound boring."

"That's not what I meant."

The cocktail waitress appeared and asked if they were hungry for a snack before the kitchen closed. Roger lifted a brow, and Caroline pulled a menu from the waitress's hand. "I think he is. Let's see."

She handed the menu to Roger and he ordered quesadillas. She had the same. They ate in near silence, talking briefly about the Astros then Carter and Abby's pending wedding plans. When they left, he walked her to her car. She fumbled with the keys, and he took them. "I'll drive you."

"How will you get back?"

"In my car."

Oh, he planned to drive *his* car. Why'd he take her keys? "But I have work tomorrow."

"I'll take you."

She knew what that meant. "No. You are *not* staying over."

He groaned. "I meant I'll come by and pick you up in the morning, *then* take you."

"In that case, okay."

He jingled the keys. "Do you have to be so difficult about everything? Sometimes just going with the flow is so much easier."

"I went with the flow, remember? It didn't work out so well." She stifled the twitter in her girlie parts that reminded her of the last time they'd been together in her place. Going with the flow in Roger's case was tempting—and dangerous.

In her driveway, he waited for her to step from the car before getting out. "Caro, do you still take pictures? I mean, now that you don't really do news articles any more, does it still interest you?"

She spoke with her back to him as she approached the door. "I take pictures for our website and blog and anything else we use to advertise. I do a lot of selfies with my phone."

Her attempt at humor had failed to impress him. She twisted her key in the lock and pushed the door open. Roger remained outside. A tinge of cold stung her shoulders. "Thanks for the ride." She rotated to give a smile. Should she hug him? Or…

Roger leaned in and kissed her. Short, sweet, and over before she expected. Nice. He hopped to the sidewalk and strode away. Why was she disappointed?

Chapter Twenty-Two

Roger thought about Caroline as he drove the short distance to retrieve her before work. Her store was obviously a compromise, and as much as she loved plants, he knew she was still searching for something. She was on her front step and stood up as he turned the car into her drive. Her store wouldn't open for another hour and half, so there was no rush.

She'd changed her hair. When had she found the time? It was still short, but the spikes were gone. Instead it curled into her cheeks and lay flat on top. "No wild-colored pants or hair today?"

She shot him a frown. "I was tired of it. Besides, change is good, right? Why are you so early?"

He jingled his keys. "Not too early, apparently, because you were waiting."

"I'd just watered my plants and was enjoying the quiet morning. I was…relaxing. You know, seizing the day."

He couldn't help himself. "I have something you can s—"

A light shriek emitted from her mouth, and she jutted her index finger at his nose. "Don't say seize. I'll call a cab, I swear."

He lifted both hands and showed his palms. "I'm not saying a word. Are you ready to go?" Until that moment, he hadn't looked at her feet. They were bare, and her toes had white polish with something painted on the big toes. She padded to the door.

"Give me five minutes." She returned in two.

She'd changed out of jeans into a skirt, without her usual leggings. It was a distraction, but he wouldn't complain. He liked the look. "I like your hair."

"Thanks." She traipsed to the car with him trailing behind.

"Nice skirt, too. Why?"

"Why not?" she snapped. She clicked the door solidly into place and crossed her arms to stop any further inquisition.

He wanted to put his hand on her head and muss the hair. She looked adorable. Like one of those little baby dolls his sisters dragged around. "I came early because I wanted to show you something before I drop you off. Is that okay?"

"As long as it's not the inside of your place."

He laughed. "Damn, and I was so hopeful you'd just jump right back into my life after all these years without any thought or hesitation."

She stared at the traffic ahead as they moved along. "You're being sarcastic."

"Yup. You're being bitchy."

That got her attention. She shifted toward him. "Sorry."

He glanced sideways and grinned. For some reason, this startled her. Her eyes popped, and she looked at the side of his face before turning to stare out the windshield. He decided to give her a few minutes and kept silent until he maneuvered the next two streets then slipped into a parking spot. Putting the car in park, he opened his door. "Hop out. This won't take long." He grabbed his camera from the backseat.

"You're taking pictures?"

He crossed to her side. "I hope so. The days are longer now, and I noticed a while back that we get a really great sunrise over the top of those trees right now. I wanted to get a couple shots." He pointed to a section of woods that edged around a park.

Caroline had a habit of wearing her emotions a little too close to the surface—it was a trait that endeared and irritated. She gasped, and her face lit up as the cloud of pinks, purples, blues, and oranges filled the morning sky. Her bursts of excitement, anger, and whatever other emotion she felt had always amused him. It drew him into her thoughts and feelings. He enjoyed and even envied the freshness of her unhidden reactions.

A flicker of light through the trees grazed his cheek. The wind was stronger than he'd anticipated. Would it affect the shots? Limbs waved and punched at the air. The light from the rising sun injected between angry foliage.

"I've always liked the sound of the wind roaring through the trees." Caroline's skirt fluttered in the breeze. She might regret that wardrobe choice soon. He doubted he would.

"It's pretty nasty this morning. I hope I can get a few good pictures. Can you grab the bag there?" He pointed at his backpack of lenses.

She grabbed the strap with her one hand and lifted. "Geeze, what do you have in here? A body?" Adding her other hand, she hoisted it like a baby and shifted the weight to one hip. "Feels like rocks."

"Camera lenses." Should he mention he'd become a little obsessed with them?

"I thought *I* was bad when it came to gadgets. By the weight of this, I'd say you're worse."

He shrugged. From experience, he'd learned to take more than expected. He never knew when he'd see something that required a different lens or a new effect.

"See, my fetishes aren't quite as obscene as you'd think." He took the bag and laid it on a nearby bench.

"That remains to be seen."

Was that a promise? The thought baffled him, and he had no response. He pointed at an outdoor slatted seat. "Sit and enjoy."

He walked a few feet and held the camera to his eye, seeking a good angle and perfect light. Snap. Snap. Snap.

"You know if you hold the button down, it will keep taking shots until you let up." Caroline's voice wasn't snarky, simply informative.

"Yes, I just wanted to try the light first. Think I have it. Now, come here."

She surveyed the primed camera. "I'm not posing."

He shook his head. "I'm not asking you to pose. I just want you to help me. I'm going to climb up, and I need you to hand this to me when I get there." He pointed to the crook of a limb that shadowed them.

Caroline bugged her eyes. "You're going to climb the tree for a picture?"

He grinned and nodded.

"Why? It's the same shot from here."

With all her experience, surely she knew that statement wasn't true. He pointed at the end of the branch where a spackling of orange-red leaves hung as if grasping their last moments of life. "Definitely not the same shot. Look at how the light comes through the thinness of those leaves and casts a rosy shadow across that patch of bark. And see the area there where something has pulled the bark away? It's almost fuchsia. I want that. In order to get it, I plan to climb."

He reached out and grabbed her hand with his free one, then plopped the camera in her palm. She looked skeptical. "When's the last time you climbed a tree?"

He hadn't thought of that. "Isn't it like riding a bicycle? You never forget. It's not that far." He stuck his foot up and hoisted himself toward the first limb. Grasping hold, he reached above and shoved to the next spot.

She lifted a hand to shield her face and squinted into the light behind the tree. The soft pink of the clouded sun added an iridescent quality to her skin. He wanted to snap a few shots of her, but knew she'd have a fit. Roger braced against the trunk and reached down. He wiggled his fingers. "Okay, pass it up here."

Caroline lifted the camera to his outstretched hand. He caught her eyes for a second, and the pink light cast a neon flicker across her irises. "You look beautiful."

She didn't look away, nor did she pull her hand free. For two seconds, he had her locked with him as the sun sparkled its early light upon them. She blinked. "You're losing your shot. If you don't hurry up, it'll be too late. You'll miss your chance." She nodded toward the horizon.

He stayed focused on her eyes. To him, her words meant something else. They meant a different chance, a different shot. "Is it too late, Caroline? Have I missed my shot?"

Moment over. The lines of her throat and neck lunged as she swallowed. "You know better than I. You're the artist."

He wasn't an artist. "That's a laugh. I wouldn't call those old snapshots art. And you know that wasn't the shot I meant."

She dropped her gaze to the landscape. "Take the picture, Rog, before it's gone. Views like that don't happen every day. And look at you: you're in a tree, wrapped around the trunk like a monkey. If you don't take it *now,* you'll have wasted a heck of an effort for nothing."

Roger turned and snapped about twenty frames, then shifted to his side and took several more. She should see the view. He wanted her to share it with him. "Come up here." He put a hand down and flicked his fingers in a come-hither gesture.

Caroline rattled her head back and forth. "I haven't climbed a tree since I was, I don't know, ten? Besides, there's no room for me."

He tied the camera strap to a limb. With his legs anchored around the trunk, he leaned down with both hands and dangled his arms. "There's plenty of room. Give me your hands. You have to see this. It's amazing."

"I'm dressed wrong." He didn't care. She hesitated, and he gestured again. Two seconds later, she reached for him. He grabbed her forearms as she wrapped her hands around his biceps and pulled her up. She was light, even lighter than his teenage sister. It took little effort to help her scramble up the trunk until she fell into his lap. Ouch. Knee to groin. "Uh, sorry."

He sucked in air and moved her a few inches. "No problem. Look." He pointed. From the ground, all one could see was trees. From this vantage point, the water of the lake on the other side shimmered like strands of tinsel, catching the light and magnifying the intensity.

Caroline glanced around, taking in the view in silence. "It's nice."

"It's better than nice." Except her weight was pinching his hip. He lifted her and shuffled her a bit to the side. The skirt hitched higher on her leg. He dared not look.

"Hey. Stop. I'll fall." She reached behind his head and clutched a limb. The simple act put her chest against his. Her heart thudded gently.

Roger wrapped his arms tightly around her tiny frame. "I won't let you fall—I have you. I'm not letting anything bad happen."

She turned slightly, and her hair fell against her cheek only centimeters away from him. It tickled. He focused on her eyes, which seemed to hold a pool of sadness. Why? "Too late for that."

Huh? "What does that mean?"

Their gazes locked for a few more seconds, then she shrugged. "Nothing."

He put a finger under her chin and pulled her face back to his. "One of the advantages of having sisters is that I'm a great listener. You know, just in case you ever feel like doing something really dumb and opening up."

"I talk."

He frowned. "I mean *really* talk. About whatever it was that put those shadows in your eyes."

Caroline lifted her chin and challenged. "My eyes are fine."

She was right about that. They *were* fine, just like all the rest of her. Every bit of her was fine—and plastered against him like a second skin. He was an idiot. This wasn't the time to dwell on her ghosts from the past. She was in his lap, watching the most vibrant sunrise he'd seen—and he was wasting the moment.

He grasped both sides of her face and searched her eyes. "Yes, they're fine…just like the rest of you." He then pulled her closer and kissed the curve of her cheek. He moved to the tip of her nose and dropped a kiss there before moving on to the other cheek. She smelled delicious, citrusy, like always. He wanted more. He dropped to her mouth, and she parted her lips to let him taste.

He still wanted more. He reached for her, trailing his fingertips along her neck then down her sides. Had she shivered? He crept his fingers down to the hem of her skirt and played with the edge. He wanted to touch her, to touch skin. So he adjusted his fingers and walked them along her leg.

"Stop." Caroline grabbed his wrist. He stilled for a second before moving his forefinger in a circular motion against her leg. Roger focused on her eyes and the feel of her skin in the morning air. It was warm to his touch, soft and trembling. He strummed softly against her thigh, and she groaned.

And closed her eyes. "Okay, don't stop."

He grinned. Don't stop. He liked the sound of *that*. Roger dropped his mouth to her neck, inhaling the scent of her skin. Something about her citrusy cleanness made him feel hopeful inside, cheerful—yet feral—a deep wildness that strained against the bands of his control. He moved his lips down the curve of her neck and deep into the V of the shirt that clung to her body. Lucky shirt. He wanted to do that—cling to her like damp silk. The thought pulled a groan from him as well.

He opened his eyes and stared through a foggy haze…at the grass below. Holy shit. He grabbed her hip, clutching onto her— panties? "We're gonna fall," he warned. The heat of her breath against his neck had made his body stiffen, betraying him when he needed to be agile. He spread his other arm and anchored against a limb, but it was too small to hold. They rolled over the bend of the branch and started to free-fall.

Caroline screamed and clutched at the bark, tearing away fragments that tumbled to the ground. Roger took a last-ditch grab at another branch, hoping it would be strong enough to save them.

It was.

Caroline crawled up him like a wild cat. Damn. Could he talk her into doing that again later? When they weren't risking life and limb in a tree? "I've got you," he whispered in her ear. "I won't let you get hurt." God, he hoped he could keep that promise.

The panic in her eyes flickered, and while Roger felt like his arms would split from his sides, he held tight. Yes, he'd keep the promise. He'd keep holding on because that's who he was. The anchor. He stared into her eyes and nodded. "You're fine."

She mirrored his nod and bit a lip. "Okay."

"Okay." They'd only descended a foot or two, thank God. "Just hold on, and I'll get us down." She wrapped around him like a koala bear, her legs tight over his hips and her arms dug into his back. As he felt the full length of her breasts and torso rubbing against the buttons on his shirt, he stifled another groan. What the hell was wrong with him?

They were about to fall from a tree, and he was—aroused. He felt like he was fifteen again. Caroline was hot—he glanced at the fingers clutching his shoulder—and totally dependent on him at the moment. He inched along until his foot could reach a lower branch.

He looked up for a second. "Damn, forgot the camera." It was still wrapped around the limb over their heads. Roger winced as Caroline dug a foot into his thigh and lifted until her breasts encompassed his face.

She yanked the camera strap loose and wrapped it over her neck. "Got it." She clutched onto his shoulder. He liked the pinch of her digging into him.

Roger nodded and worked slowly, finding one foothold, then another, until he had them near the ground. Caroline unwrapped her legs from his waist and dropped.

A rush of cold—and loneliness?—enveloped Roger.

"I should get to work." Caroline pulled a leaf from her hair.

"Or not," Roger offered.

Chapter Twenty-Three

Caroline eyed him suspiciously. Mr. Reliable wanted her to ditch work? No way. "What do you mean?"

Roger slipped his hands into his pockets then shrugged and kicked the leaves they'd knocked loose. "You could be a few minutes late, couldn't you?"

"Why would I want to do that?"

He grinned. "I thought we might finish what we started without the altitude problems."

What was it about those silly dimples that made her insides curl up in a little ball and start spinning like a roly-poly? She stared. It had to be the little boy in him. He was built like a man and talked like one, but his face was young and...a tad devilish. He was likely one of those children best remembered for playing pranks on teachers. Were his sisters dimpled like that, too?

"Abby will be alone and swamped. I can't do that to her. We're partners."

"Maybe, but what if it's a slow morning? You won't be missed at all."

She considered the thought. "Um, let me call and check."

He looked up at the sky, and she wondered if he was praying for slow business. She hoped not; they needed the money. Of course, she needed a little more of what they'd started, too, but sometimes you have to take what you can get.

Abby picked up on the first ring—meaning the store was empty. "Hey, what's up?"

Caroline hesitated. "Mind if I'm a little late today?"

"Not at all. It's dead here right now. I was just thinking about reorganizing the shelves." Yikes—that meant the store wasn't just dead; it was comatose.

After saying goodbye, Caroline hung up and turned to Roger. "Hmmm, guess you have me captive a little longer."

• • •

"Captive" wasn't exactly the word he'd have used, but at least they had a few more minutes. Caroline glanced up at the tree they'd nearly fallen from. Her neck arched gracefully, and he wanted to run a finger down the soft lines. She dropped her glance to meet his. "Where'd you learn to use the camera like that, seriously?"

"What? You think you're the only one with talent? I have talent, too…"

She huffed. "I *saw* that. And despite the fact that you had an unwilling subject and no signed release to use those photos of me, I have to admit they were good. Better than good, they were unusual. Artistic. Do you have others like that?"

Others of her? Or another girl's body? What was she inferring? "Not like those. Those were a one-time attempt at…something. I don't know. But where did I learn to use the camera? From you at first. I took a few photography night classes after I graduated and realized pretty quickly there was a lot more to it than just clicking the button. Now, I look for shadows. Not gradual ones—for deep, dark shadows that really make a scene dramatic. That tree's a good example. If you look through the leaves, you get this veiled glow of green and yellow. Then there are these vivid oranges and reds. Let me show you."

He shifted the camera and slid open the review screen. After a few movements, he turned the display to show her the shots of the tree. Green leaves that faded to red and revealed the crevices of the bark on the side, then the sunlight glowing through with streaks of brightness. Bold pinks and oranges. Soothing greens and browns.

She focused on the screen. "Oh. That's beautiful. What do you do with them? Do you blow them up and frame them like the ones at the fundraiser?"

He shrugged. "Wouldn't that be nice to get that much money for each of these? No, I upload some of them to this stock photo website where they pay me if the pictures get downloaded. A lot of them just get deleted because I usually take a dozen or so just to get a good shot."

She handed the camera back. "I know the feeling. So, how'd you meet my father?"

He wanted to tell the full details, but some things are just too painful. Would she understand the effect her mother had on those around her? Would she get angry? "I met your father through your mother."

Her eyes popped at the words. "What? My mother's…gone."

Roger's stomach turned as if someone had kicked him, a quick reminder to choose his words carefully. Still, she needed to know. "Your mother was in one of the photography classes I took. She wanted to capture the people around her in the hospital. According to her, it was something she could do that didn't require becoming a painter or a seamstress. I had no idea at the time you two were connected. Of course, as soon as I learned her name, I asked. You favor her a little. More than a little, I guess."

"Was this a one-night class?"

"No, it was a six-week class that met at the library. She stopped coming after the fourth class, and by that time, I'd become so used to her chatter that I called to find out if she was okay. Until then, I had no idea she was sick. She always seemed tired, but, well, you don't ask people personal questions when you don't know them. Even if you do, they don't always tell the truth. Some do. Some don't. With your mother, it seemed rude to ask. Your father answered the phone and told me she had gone back to the hospital. So…I went to visit her."

Caroline's eyes glittered in the morning sun, and he knew there was a depth of emotion behind her blinking and stillness. "You did? I hated that hospital."

He nodded. "Can't blame you. Not a pleasant place."

"Was that before or after I came back?"

"Before."

"Why didn't she tell me about you? She could have—"

"She talked about you, but I never told her we'd already met. I just acted…" He shrugged because he wasn't sure what to say. Carol had been pretty out of it at the time and showed him a pile of pictures Caroline sent home. Good pictures. Sad ones, too. It made his work seem trivial. She was snapping death, war, and all sorts of violence. He was snapping lights, fences, faces, and abstract nothings.

Caroline lifted her head, closed her eyes, and held still as the sun beamed upon her still silhouette. Seconds ticked by, but Roger dared not interrupt her thoughts because they seemed a tribute to her mother. Her shoulders rose and lowered as she drew in a deep breath and sighed. "Thank you for being there."

"I just talked to her a few times. I wasn't really around much, and then you were home. I thought you'd be upset, so I stopped."

"Did she take the pictures she planned? Have you seen them?"

He wasn't sure she'd like the answer. "Yes."

"Can I see them?"

"I don't have them. Talk to your father. All I've seen are the ones he submitted for the fundraiser."

She blinked, clearly confused. "She had pictures at the fundraiser, too? Really?"

He nodded. "That's why I took you."

Caroline cursed. "I was so upset that I missed them."

It was probably better that way, considering the pictures weren't just snapshots her mother had taken of random people or things. Carol's photographs were a tribute in some way to her daughter's work, her husband's work, and—death. They haunted him sometimes.

"Ask your dad then." Roger's phone chirped in his pocket, and he felt a surge of relief for the interruption. He lifted the device to his ear and spoke.

Relief turned to a stiff pinch in his neck, which he rubbed fervently as his sister railed on him about their father's new family. Hell. "I can't talk right now, Rhi. Can I call you back later?"

Caroline lifted a brow.

He ignored her questioning glance as his sister spoke. "Oh, you're busy."

"Yep, I'll call you later, okay?" He snapped the phone back into his pocket. "Sorry about that."

His phone sprang into action again. He yanked it from the depths of his pants. Same number. "What?" Could she hear the aggravation in the tone?

"They're at the hospital, in case you wanted to know. Something about complications with the pregnancy. They're running tests."

Shit. "Oh, sorry. Okay, I'll go. Are you there?"

"Uh-uh. I'm working. I can't."

"Is Mom there?"

A snort burned his ear. "Are you kidding?"

She was right—it was a dumb question. "Why should I go?"

Another snort. "Because someone has to. He would want you."

Roger growled. "What if I don't—"

"Just go." The phone clicked and went silent. Fine.

"I have to go to the hospital. My dad's wife has something going on. She's pregnant."

"Why *you* and not him?"

Roger gathered the photography equipment. "Oh, he's there already. Apparently he just wants company. She's having complications or something. I don't know."

Caroline pulled one of the bags from his grasp and lifted it over her shoulder. "I'm sorry."

He strode to the vehicle and stowed the equipment then started after her to get the door. "The whole thing is screwed up."

She squinted up at him. "Aren't we all?"

"In some ways, yes. Not like this though. Your family had issues, but they were out of your control. Out of their control. This is different. At least your parents continued to love each other."

She slid into the seat and pulled the door closed. "It wasn't really in your control either, was it? People choose to love or not love."

Good point. But it *had* been in his father's control, and that was the problem. That was what burned his ass. The question blasted through his head for the ten millionth time. What kind of grown man *chooses* to ditch a wife with four kids?

Chapter Twenty-Four

Walking into another hospital was as attractive as swimming with sharks, but somehow Caroline was padding along behind Roger as he approached the nurse's station. In the maternity ward was an overpowering smell of baby powder—a nice alternative to the antiseptic smells she'd encountered when visiting her mother.

The doctor approached with a smile—not a pasted-on look that inferred bad news, but a genuinely pleasant smile. He liked his job. "You're with the Freemans? They're at the end on the right."

Roger nodded and trudged toward the room. He turned. "Wait. Is everything okay? You know, with the kid?"

The doctor snickered. "It's not really a kid yet, but yes. He'll be fine. She's just a little anemic. We'll keep an eye on her, but nothing looks out of place."

Caroline noticed Roger's jaw twitch. "*He?* It's a boy?"

The doctor winked. "Oops. Don't tell them. They didn't want to know."

Roger's face softened. "Wow, a brother. What d'ya know. Poor little sucker. He's doomed."

Caroline punched his arm. "Aren't you happy for them?" A sibling would have been her dream…a gift, actually.

He shrugged. "I guess. As long as no one asks me to babysit or change his shorts. I don't do diapers—or babies."

She thought about that for a second. She could see him with kids. Hell, he *was* a kid half the time. She patted his arm. "You'll be great. I can just see you with a baby-blue diaper bag over one shoulder and your camera stuff over the other. It'll be a new subject for those photos of yours."

He turned and frowned. "It? Don't you mean he?"

She shrugged and followed him into the room. "Whatever. Just make sure you don't spill the beans and ruin it for them."

Inside, the room instantly felt chilly. One could cut the strain between Roger and his father with a knife. Caroline rolled her shoulders and watched Roger talk with the older version of himself. When he was satisfied that he'd performed his duty as an attentive son, they left.

"I take it you two aren't on best of terms?" she asked as they took the elevator down to the first floor.

"Why'd you ask?"

"I don't know. Maybe the clipped two-sentence conversations. "Yes, sir. No, sir. Glad you're okay. I've never seen you so formal. So…rude. Why'd you visit if you don't like her?"

Roger leveled a cold stare on Caroline, and she shivered. He'd never looked at her in such a sterile way before. "I don't care one way or the other about her. But think about it, Caro. If your father had left your mother for someone almost half his age, leaving you to raise the rest of your siblings because he suddenly decided he needed freedom—would you be okay with that?"

Her stomach tightened. While her father hadn't left for another woman, he might as well have. He'd still gone away when she was a child. He'd still deserted her, deserted them. So, while she didn't completely feel the same, she certainly understood the hurt and frustration.

He pulled his keys from a pocket and pressed the unlock button. The vehicle beeped twice. "What difference does it make? You don't get it. He *left*. Not just my mother…all of us. Do you—"

She jogged to his side and grabbed his arm. "Hey. Stop for a minute."

He turned, his brown eyes deep and brooding. "What? Are you going to tell me to forgive him? To get over it and be happy for them? If you are, go to hell. I don't need you to tell me how to handle my family, Caroline. I don't need your advice."

If he'd said that years ago, she'd have lit into him and ranted. But things change, and her temper had dampened. She knew his resentment; she'd felt it herself. "No, I *do* get it. I mean, my father may not have left for a woman, but he *did* leave. He left for his job. He wasn't even here the first time my mother was ill, and I barely remembered him as a kid. He'd come back with gifts, like that was supposed to make it okay. It didn't because he'd just leave again. So, I just wanted to say…I don't really know exactly how you feel, but I *do* get it. I'm sorry you had to deal with that."

He blinked. He blinked again. Was he unsure what to stay? Had she baffled him?

"Thank you."

The stone in her stomach dislodged a little. She couldn't miss the opportunity to tease. "You're welcome—big brother." She grinned.

"Don't push it." Roger slipped an arm around her waist. He tugged her close, and Caroline thudded against his chest. Her chin met his breastplate. "Oops, sorry. That was a bit rough."

She shrugged. "I can do rough."

He lifted a brow and peered down into her gaze. "I like the sound of that."

Caroline smiled then tiptoed her fingers around the back of his neck and yanked his mouth to hers. With their lips crushed together, she mumbled, "I thought you would."

He slid his other hand around her and splayed it across the small of her back, then walked her backward until he'd captured her against the hood of his vehicle. Caroline's back arched as he bent over her, his mouth exploring hers. The warmth of his breath tickled her neck as he trailed kisses down the curve of her chin, then along her throat and even lower. "You smell delicious."

She heard giggles as a couple of hospital staff trekked past them to a vehicle. "Anything smells good after being in a hospital. You make me sound like dessert."

"You are." Roger lifted his head and looked through lidded eyes as the passersby climbed into a car and left. His cell sounded off in his pocket, breaking the moment. "I should take you to work now, I guess."

Bummer. She wasn't ready to go. Not with his arms encasing her in the coziest of hugs and his mouth exploring parts of her that needed further review. Of course, they were in a parking lot—in full view. "Okay."

Apparently he wasn't ready to go either because he dropped back into a super-hot and wet kiss that curled her toes and made little somersaults deep in her gut. Fifteen minutes later, Caroline was sure she hadn't a stitch of lipstick left on her mouth, and though her hair might not be spiky, it had to be standing on end. Those kisses were too wild to leave any part of her flat.

Roger cleared his throat. "Well, okay then. I guess we leave now."

He opened the door for her, and she melted into the seat of his SUV. When he slid in beside her, he jumbled his keys and dropped them. Was he as rattled as she was? He retrieved the keys and met her bewildered gaze. "Sorry, I just guess I'm a little surprised."

Surprise wasn't the word she'd have used, but okay. "Why?"

He flashed the dimples for a second. "I had forgotten the wildness of you. I…missed that."

Wildness? They drove the few miles to her store, and he pulled to the curve, shut the car off, and circled to open her door. She stepped out and began to protest. "I never thought of myself as wild, per se. I was never—"

He looked up at the sky. "Don't read anything into the words, Caroline. I don't mean crazy or like a party animal. I just mean… passionate." He hooked an index finger from her to him. "This wasn't the way I thought it would be."

"What exactly did you think, then?"

"Nothing. Don't worry about it." He turned her toward the shop door and gave her a slight shove. "Go to work."

So, he apparently thought her passionate and apparently that was a bad thing? Why? Because he wanted her gone as quickly as possible? She shook her head. Confusing. She opened her mouth to speak, and three words came to mind—*kiss my ass*. Not passionate. Not even close.

"I'm cooking spaghetti tonight in case, you know, you get hungry after work," Roger said.

The angry embers in her gut dampened. "I don't get off work until eight. I'm closing."

He jingled his keys and dimpled up. "Funny, I usually don't eat until eight thirty or nine at night. I work out after I leave the office."

Hmmm. Interesting. "I like pasta."

Chapter Twenty-Five

Caroline donned a black cap before she left for his house. It wasn't cold, but the cap helped cover her growing fringed bangs. Roger yanked open the door, sending a cloud of steam and garlic to greet her. She drew in the scent and smiled. A man who cooked. Where had he been all her life? She followed into his kitchen and took a seat at a bar stool against the counter. He'd been right here—less than an hour from the place they'd met years ago. *She* was the one who had disappeared, not him. She had to *go find herself*—that's what she'd told him.

The weight of that decision haunted her. Why? Because the answer was no closer all these years later than when she'd made her escape. "It must be wonderful."

His eyes met hers. "It's just spaghetti. I doubt it's all that wonderful."

A big bulk of a dog lumbered to her side and nuzzled against her legs. She looked down into velvety-brown eyes. "Oh my God, is that Conan?"

He nodded.

She ran a hand over his head, and his tail thumped the wall beside them. "Look at you, buddy. You're getting a little gray here and there, but you're still kicking. Way to go, big guy."

The dog yawned a funny nasal response. "He's half-blind and his legs tend to give out once in a while, but I don't have the heart to put him down."

Caroline frowned. "Don't you dare! See, *this* is what I meant by wonderful—you've always known exactly what you wanted and where you'd be. You've always known who you are. Look at you, you're still—"

"Predictable?"

"That wasn't where I was going. Strong, supportive, maybe even driven. You've accomplished something with your life. Unlike me."

He pulled a pan from the stove and poured the contents over a colander. A cloud of puffy steam filled the air. He reared back to keep from singeing his face. "Yeah, I live in a fifty-year-old house with an ancient dog whose best talent is hogging the couch. Plus don't forget my exciting job that's not so exciting. Big accomplishment."

"At least you know who you are and who you want to be."

He dumped the pasta into a bowl and lowered the pan into the sink. The aluminum bottom sizzled against the water underneath. He leaned over and pulled the felt cap from her head and tousled her hair. "You changed your hair. Why?"

Hell if she knew. "I can't seem to find a style that jazzes me and speaks to my inner being."

"I didn't know hair had a voice." He thrust his fingers into her bangs and pushed them away from her forehead. "It jazzes me though. Funny, I would have never pictured you this way back then. You always had it up in some headband or tied back. I hadn't imagined it cut short, but it suits you."

She blinked and moved her eyes to the window. "Yeah, I cut it off on a whim when I was in Teslehad. There was an uprising there that got a little ugly. I hid out for a few days hoping it would calm down, and there were these kids. They all had cut theirs off—you couldn't tell who was female and who wasn't. I looked around and quickly realized if I was going to blend into the background and report about what those people faced, I'd better *blend in.* So, I cut it off."

"The girls cut their hair to look like boys?"

Caroline nodded and watched the thick red sauce bubble and pop as he added more garlic then tossed in some green spices. A flash of red popped over the edge of the pan to the floor. That would leave a mess. "It was safer."

His lips pursed as he stirred the sauce with a wooden spoon. That bothered him? Was he angry? She watched his movements in silence, unsure what to say next. His hands were thick and strong. Watching him soothed her. Roger reached to a cabinet and pulled out two stemmed glasses. "Wine okay with you?"

"Definitely okay."

The ruby liquid gurgled defiantly as it flowed from its bottled home into the glasses. He smiled as his eyes met her. Caroline cringed. It wasn't the normal dimpled warmth that promised an undertone of wicked sensuality. It was threaded with kindness and understanding, the type of smile one gives a person who's gone through significant loss. She didn't want that smile. He held out the glass for her to take.

"Don't give me that look." She pulled the wine from his grasp and took a long sip.

"What look? I wasn't—"

"It's filled with sympathy. I don't need sympathy." She cast a glance down at her body, holding her arms up for view. "I'm still here with all my body parts. There's nothing wrong with me, so don't look at me like I belong in a psych ward or need PTSD counseling."

He pulled a sip from his glass and narrowed his eyes. When he finally put the glass down, she could have cut the silence with a butter knife. He opened a cabinet, pulled out some dishes, and placed one in front of her. "If you got all that from one look, then I suck at body language. Drink your wine, Caro, and don't read anything into my words—or lack of words. Just loosen up and be here, right here with me."

She bit her lip and stared at the pasta. He was right: she'd taken one look and jumped to conclusions. Like she often did around people who knew where she'd been and the mess she'd made of her life. He wasn't one of those people though—she'd never told him. They'd stopped speaking long before she'd made the trek to Teslehad. "I'm sorry."

Caroline poked her fork into the plate of steaming tomato sauce and twisted the noodles around the prongs. Her appetite was gone. The enticing aroma of garlic and parmesan was overshadowed by the chill that ran across her shoulder blades.

"No need. Listen, I have no idea what you've been through or why you think I'd have that *look*. I just—"

She had to tell him. "Abby and I met over there. She was with her brother on a post-grad vacation. We instantly drew to each other, partly because we were Americans and, well, who wouldn't? She's great. I left Abby in Scotland because there was a bulletin on the newswire underground that a skirmish was beginning near Teslehad. They wanted coverage—anything they could get. I thought, here's my big chance to show them I can be a real journalist. I could report important news as it occurred."

Roger focused on his spaghetti and forked a bite, rolled the pasta twice, then slipped it through his lips. After swallowing, he grabbed his wine glass and stared at the remaining liquid. "You don't have to tell me anything, you know."

He lifted the glass and sipped. She followed his lead and took a drink. "I want to—no, I *need* to tell. It. Haunts me."

His silence served as an awkward acknowledgment to continue if she wished. She sucked in a breath of courage and let the words softly flow. "When I arrived, the town was already under siege. It was small and remote. Maybe a few hundred people if you counted the ones who spent most of their time playing soldier."

The gurgle of spaghetti spinning on his fork broke a moment of silence as she considered her next words. "I took a lot of pictures. Stills of the town. Shots of the people wandering around, a couple of teenage boys with guns slung over their shoulders, and a group of kids playing soccer in the street with a busted ball. It was like a *National Geographic* panoramic."

"But no skirmish?"

She shook her head and chewed. Slinging a mouthful of wine back, she set down her glass and reached for the bottle. After pouring them the last of the wine, she spoke. "Not that I could see. But they watched me all the time so I was careful not to act suspicious. I cut my hair to blend in, I wore old clothes that I'd bought off a local, I only used my press ID when things became…"

Ugly.

"Caroline." His voice was soft, like a cotton blanket after a hot shower. Was he urging her to stop? Or continue?

"I wanted the story. I had no idea they were rounding the kids up for execution—I thought it was all a game. These little kids ran around kicking the ball, playing, completely unaware they were being drawn in as targets. More and more arrived, and it seemed like a nice little human interest story."

Roger cleared his throat with a guttural double-hitch. "Where were you when this went on? Were you playing with them?" Was there concern hidden in his words?

She wagged her head again in denial. "I stood in a window on the corner of the street and snapped photos. I…laughed. They were grinning and running. Right up until the gunshots rattled away."

Caroline shoved her fist against her mouth and pressed hard. She clenched her eyes. "They shot the older ones first. It was like they didn't have the stomach for the little ones, or at least not at first. I will never forget. This one little boy curled around his sister, wrapping her up like he was a turtle shell. He…tried to save her."

Roger had stopped eating. He ran a forefinger along the stem of his glass as he listened. She knew he wanted to ask about the boy, so she answered. "He failed."

Caroline lifted her eyes to Roger's. Her eyelids burned. "They shot him seventeen times. His body was cut nearly in two; the last shots pierced her chest and skull. You know why they killed those little kids?" She lifted her chin.

"Why?" Roger's chair creaked as he turned to face her.

Caroline's shoulders shuddered as she pulled in another painful breath. She wasn't sure if she could tell the next part. She'd never said it out loud.

"Look at me." His hands heated her cheeks as he palmed her face and pulled her gaze to meet his. "Tell me."

"They *wanted* me to see it, to report it. They wanted the attention. They'd watched me for days and knew who I was. All that time, I thought I'd kept a low profile. I hadn't. They baited me. The man who killed those kids had spoken to me the day before. He could have easily done the same to—"

"You." The word reverberated in the silence between them. Roger thumbed her cheeks, whisking the water from her lower lids. It comforted her.

She stared into the depths of his brown eyes. He must think her a coward for not stopping it. "I just watched them die. I *took pictures of the entire thing.*"

The scent of Roger's cologne filled her nose as he pulled her tight against his chest and nestled her forehead against his chin. "What else *could* you do, babe? That was your job. You did your job."

"I killed them, Roger." Her voice flat-lined, barely registering the sweet nickname. She'd said it for the first time. She'd admitted her part.

Chapter Twenty-Six

The pasta sat like lead in Roger's stomach. He strummed his fingers over the soft wisps of Caroline's hair. His shirt was damp where her tear-stained cheeks had soaked the fabric, but he didn't care. It was time for a wash anyway.

His problems were trivial compared to the burdens Caroline dragged around inside. Financial woes meant nothing. His sisters' drama, his mother's whining, his father's pending child—they were miniscule in comparison. How could she possibly believe their deaths were her fault?

"You're kidding, right?" He tried to keep his voice as deadpan, but anger sizzled somewhere deep inside him. It threatened to boil over.

Caroline cleared her throat with a gurgled cough. Her eyes flashed. "Of course I'm not kidding. Why the hell would I joke about people dying?"

He realized his poor choice of words and let out a nervous laugh. Leaning back to focus on her watery pupils, he softened his voice. "Hey, hey. I didn't mean the story wasn't true. But surely you don't believe you're responsible for what happened? Caro, there's no explanation for that kind of brutality, and had you not been there, someone else would have. It still would have happened. Nothing would have changed—it just wouldn't have been *you*."

She thudded her head against his collarbone, breathing in his scent. "Forgive me, but I think I could live with that."

"You're a hero."

Caroline dropped her feet to the floor and shoved away. Grabbing her plate, she carried it to the sink and flipped on the faucet. The hiss of water stirred the room. "That's ridiculous.

There's nothing heroic about what happened over there. I didn't do anything. I lived. They died. Those little kids are the heroes."

She was wrong about that. They were victims—or scapegoats. He supposed in some sick way that was heroic. "Reporting what happened is heroic."

Her hands shook the tiniest bit as she swirled a scrubber over her dish then placed it in the washer. "That's just it—I didn't report anything. I wrote the story, and then I was scared shitless and told them to shelve it. I was afraid. Then my mother got sick, which gave me an excuse to come home and leave it all behind. To pretend it never happened."

Wouldn't it have been nice had it not happened? Where would they be now had she stayed? "But it did. You can't change your past, kiddo. Your future's wide open, but not the past. The sooner you find a way to deal with it, the sooner you'll get on with the good stuff."

"I don't even know what the good stuff is, Rog. I'm not like you—I thought I had a gift. I thought I was meant to be a journalist. I haven't a clue what to do with myself now. I'm a… mess."

He wished he could take all of those memories out of her head and burn them into oblivion. Erase them somehow. "Not a mess. Just human like the rest of us."

She tossed her gaze skyward before giving him one of her don't-shit-me looks. "Human like the rest of us? I don't see you still trying to figure out who you are. Nope. *You* have all the answers—like always."

She really thought that? "Right. I'm the answer man. Ask me anything. I can tell fortunes. I can plan your future and make everything perfect." His voice was laced with sarcasm. He waved a hand at their surroundings. "That's why I have all these riches and am constantly surrounded by adoring fans. Come on, Caroline. No one, and I mean *no one,* has a perfect life. We're always searching for something. Or someone. And guess what? We all have *shit* to deal with. Some of us more than others. Sometimes it's big like yours, sometimes not so much. All of us wish for more than we possess and strive to be better than we are. To *find* ourselves."

Caroline stared at him and blinked. She opened her mouth to speak, but said nothing. Instead she lifted her head and arched her neck until it popped, then lowered back to meet his gaze. "Yeah, well, find your ass over here at the sink with a towel will you? I need someone to help me clean up this mess. And by the way, you have spaghetti sauce on you."

Drama over—just like that. Thank God. Only he knew it wasn't really over. It would never be. He couldn't care less about the sauce. "You don't have to do that."

She gave him that look again, stuffed to the seams with disbelief. "My mother had one very strict rule about the kitchen, and I've stuck with it faithfully: the cook never cleans. If someone is gracious enough to feed me, the least I can do is clean for them." She ran her gaze over the mass of sauce-spattered pans. "Of course, Mom had never seen a mess like this when she made that rule."

"Masterpieces sometimes get messy." Not that he'd call his spaghetti a masterpiece.

Caroline's cheek bulged as she tucked her tongue into the hollow. Was she stifling a laugh? "Um, it *was* good, but unless you have more recipes in your repertoire, don't quit your day job anytime soon."

"Come on now. It might not smell like a store full of flowers, but who can't get into garlic?"

She didn't stifle her laugh this time. She held up her hands, palms up, and seesawed them. It was repressed emotion but who cared? "Hmm, garlic or flowers. Let me think about that—tough decision."

He smiled, a puzzled half-lift of lips. Her face flashed color and warmed. She'd shoved her baggage into the closet of her mind and come back to him. Thank God.

Wait.

Came back to him? Had he wanted her to come back? As much as he liked being with her like this again, something inside him clicked. He knew he had to help her. Worse, the only way to help was something he wasn't sure he'd be able to do.

He had to make her go back and finish what she'd started.

Chapter Twenty-Seven

A door slammed and footsteps plodded across the carpet. The heavy clip of a person on a mission. "Hey, you here? It smells like heaven. Did you order Italian?" Roger's sister Rebecca rounded the corner and stopped at the entry to his kitchen. "Oh, hi." Rebecca glanced at the soapsuds on Caroline's elbows. She grabbed a towel from the counter and tossed it to her.

Before his sister said anything further, he'd better clear up the confusion. "I cooked spaghetti. There's a little left." He pointed toward the bowl. Thankfully, she chose not to make a snarky comment about how rarely he cooked. Instead, she yanked open the silverware drawer and pulled out a fork.

Rebecca rounded the counter and plopped down on Roger's stool before jamming her fork into the small pile of pasta. "Wow, not bad. You really *can* cook. Who knew?" There she went. So much for holding back.

Roger sighed. He wasn't in the mood for a family night at the moment. "What are you doing here?"

Rebecca nodded at Caroline and spoke between mouthfuls. "Need your help. My calculus class is kicking my ass. I was fine until a couple of weeks ago, then bam—he threw a curveball at us." She turned toward Caroline and waved. "Hi!"

You're kidding me. "Now? Can't you see I'm busy?"

Caroline wiped her hands on her back pockets and introduced herself. She held out a hand, and the two shook. "It's fine," Caroline said. "I was pretty good at calc at one point. What are you working on now?"

"You're the decorator? I thought you were—" Roger knew what was coming next. Blonde. He had to stop her.

"Caroline and I knew each other in college. She's a partner in the new florist business downtown."

Recognition flitted across Rebecca's features, an almost unseen quirk to her eyes. Roger hoped Caroline hadn't noticed her confusion. "Oh, cool. Here. Look at this, then." Rebecca slid a paper in front of her then twisted in her chair and winked. "I have a question, brother."

Uh-oh. What next?

"You have a butcher knife in your hand, and she," Rebecca pointed at Caroline, "has red goo all over her shirt. I didn't show up for some kind of slasher scene, did I?"

Roger stared at the knife, which he'd intended to toss into the washer. A cackle came from the table; he shifted his gaze toward the two women and blinked. The cackle turned into a howl, and Caroline wiped her eyes. From tears to hysterics in thirty seconds flat. "What's so funny?"

Caroline pointed—at his crotch. He looked down to see a blob of spaghetti sauce that was now permanently embedded over his privates.

Rebecca chortled. "Just asking: Are you still able to have kids at some point in the future? I just want to make sure our wonderful lineage doesn't end with you. That would be a crime."

Roger put the knife in the dishwasher, wet a towel, and attempted to clean himself. The end result was worse. He now had a *huge* soaking-wet spot surrounding the red stain. Great. "Don't worry. Dad took care of that for us. Seems our new addition is a boy."

Rebecca gasped. "What? So the baby's okay? I thought—I—oh, shit. Don't tell Dad, but I sort of thought she'd lost it. Why did I jump to conclusions? That's *awful*."

Roger frowned. "Nice of you. No, she's fine, just a little anemic—and very pregnant with your baby brother."

"That's *half*-brother, and don't forget he's yours, too. Kinda makes you feel young again doesn't it?"

That wasn't what it made him feel at all, but he'd keep the conversation PG. "Watch your tongue, young lady. Oh, and by the way, Dad doesn't know it's a boy—they wanted to be surprised. I told him you were thrilled and couldn't wait to babysit for them."

Rebecca stuck out her tongue and pointed both eyes at her nose. "Creep."

Caroline cleared her throat. "Okay, so I think I remember what all this is about—on your paper, I mean. Let me show you."

The two girls buried their heads in calculus as Roger finished the dishes. He enjoyed listening to their voices; it reminded him of when the whole family lived under one roof and his father was still…his father. Those days were gone, just like the days of seeing his mother happy.

The clincher was that things would need to get a lot worse before they got better. While the two women gelled over equations, Roger plotted in his mind how he'd deal with his new discovery. How could he help Caroline while still managing the family finances? It would be a hell of a lot easier to simply take his dad's route and leave.

But he wasn't a quitter.

• • •

Opening up for the first time felt like pulling the plug from a bathtub full of water. Was this similar to what an AA meeting feels like for an addict? Tides of emotion rushed over Caroline, pulling her to tell more, to learn more. Once she had exposed her darker side to Roger, she felt a need to confront her father. He'd tried to talk to her about it once, but she'd dissed him. She still had a lot of anger to overcome.

An open box of flowers waiting to be removed and displayed sat beside her as she stared at the computer screen. She had no idea where to begin, so she just…typed.

Daisies, Dads, and Do-Overs

*I sit here staring at a box of flowers that want, no, **need** to be placed on display for our customers. They're my favorite and quite beautiful in the most simplistic way: daisies. DAISIES. Only three colors— yellow, green, and white—but they complement each other perfectly and smile at the world with an internal scrappiness that only comes from a plant devoid of delicacy. Devoid of delicacy, you ask? Yes, that's right. Daisies were originally (and still are) weeds to a farmer. They take over fields and crops so that soon you have nothing but a field full of flowers. They're stronger than a brick fortress and can grow and thrive in virtually any habitat. I've always thought of myself as having the strength of a daisy, but a few years ago that strength was tested and now I'm selling…daisies. I'll circle back to that story in a minute.*

One major source of strength in my life has been the impact my mother had on my youth. She passed away after an illness a few years ago. Until then, she'd been my primary caregiver because my father was gone. Not gone as in deceased, just…absent. I wasn't sure why or when it all started, but he was a journalist and on assignment during my teen years and later. My mother never explained it to me and talked as if he'd return any day. Yet he didn't. I stopped expecting him when I left for college.

Recently, though, he reentered my life. And with my mother gone, it's been—interesting. Memorial Day is coming soon, and I wanted to mention him because he won a well-known literary award a few years ago for an article about Korean War veterans. It exposed the deficits in our public health system's ability to care for disabled vets. He was obsessed with the story for years. Now, after reading that story and my father's subsequent book…I hate them both. They were the mistress. The other woman. The replacement for me and my mother.

Yes, I realize I shouldn't air my dirt publicly, but…come on, Dad. You could have at least cared enough to take us along on your dream quest, couldn't you?

So, people, I ask you: is there anything in your life you wish you could DO OVER? For me, there are several, but the two that stare me in the mirror every day are these:

1. *Could I go back and make him love me enough to take me, too?*
2. *I let a mass of children die while trying to please him by following in his footsteps.*

I can explain this one. It's the most important part of this message because…

She stopped typing and read over the words two or three times, knowing she hadn't the guts to publish such a bombshell. Regardless, it felt good to put the words to paper and voice a miniscule piece of her discontent. She was sure debating whether to continue when the door to the stockroom flung open.

Caroline jolted and slammed her hands against the keys, shoving the keyboard off the desk. "Holy crap—warn me before you fly through here like a bomber plane."

Abby grinned in mischievous pleasure. "Oops. What're you doing?"

Caroline leveled her gaze on the blank computer screen. She must have shut it off accidentally. "Well, I *was* writing this week's blog until you blasted in here. I'll have to start over later, as it looks like I lost my post when I dropped the keyboard." She placed the board gingerly in place and pushed away from the desk. "Did you need me?"

Abby sucked in her cheeks to stifle a grin and continued in her "business voice." "Yes. I believe it's time we discussed the store's plans for the upcoming holidays. Maybe you could blog about those? Valentine's is over, but we have Easter, Memorial Day, and all the rest. I've given a little thought to—"

Caroline felt the infection of her excitement as it coursed from Abby like magic dust from the good fairy. "You're really into this, aren't you?"

Abby's eyes rounded as she bobbled her head up and down. Holy shop-mania, she looked crazy-giddy. Her voice skated into a high-pitched song. "I love being able to support myself without my family's interference. It's…awesome."

Was she hugging herself? Caroline rolled her eyes. "Yeah, I'll bet that family interference is a real pain in the ass," she snapped. Without another word, she rose from her chair and strode past Abby, who stood with her mouth agape.

It was a mean thing to say, and her regret manifested as a massive headache, but she continued out of the store and went for coffee. Abby deserved a partner who was into their business—focused and excited. Like her. *All I seem to do is live in the past with my demons.*

•••

Roger sat and pretended to focus on the work strewn across his office desk. In truth, his mind whirled around the list he'd made the night before, after Caroline left. The first item taunted him—did he have the balls to make the call?

He lifted his phone from his pocket, but it burst into action before he touched a key. The number looked familiar, although he couldn't place it. He answered.

"Roger? Abby here. I've done something terrible, and I need your advice." Her voice was staccato and breathless with panic.

"Are you hurt? Wait, is Carter okay? You're not—"

"No, no. Nothing like that. He's fine—we're both fine—although I think I've done something terrible to Caroline. She wrote this blog post today that was more than disturbing, but I only looked at the title and didn't bother to read the rest. The computer had flickered off when I startled her, and I thought she was finished. It was sitting at the 'post' prompt, so what was I supposed to do? She had walked out."

What? "She walked out? She quit?"

He heard music in the background, probably their speakers at the store. Caroline exhaled into the phone. "No, of course not. Why would she do that? We're partners. No, she got mad at me after I bragged about my family. It was stupid. That's not the issue. I posted the post…only now I don't think she intended it to post. And, oh my God, it's posted. The whole world is going to read it, her *dad* will read it, and—oh shit, here she comes. Call me back. Okay?"

He stared at the phone in awe of the crazy woman on the other end of the conversation. "Okkkaaayyy."

Out of curiosity, he clicked the link on his desktop—and gasped. He read down the page, letting the revelation creep over him. Then he gave a double fist-pump in the air. *Way to go, girl.* Finally, she'd said what he knew she wanted to say all along. Accidentally, albeit, but it was out. He read back over and thought for a second. Well, at least he wouldn't need to have a sit-down with her father.

The screen refreshed, and he read the first comments. Holy shit. More comments. People asking for the details and wanting to know more. Hell, the fact that she'd put those words on the page was a huge step toward building herself back to the girl he knew. He doubted she was ready to spill further. Abby was right: there's no way Caroline would have posted that post. She must have written it for herself, expecting to delete it. Thanks to Abby, her personal therapy had just turned into an episode of the Kardashians, complete with some serious parent bashing.

Roger grabbed his keys and strode from the office. He wasn't sure what he'd do but knew she would need support. No need to call Abby since the store was only a few minutes away.

He whisked the car into the fifteen-minute customer parking and shoved through the door. "Where is she?"

Abby's head throttled back and forth. "She grabbed her purse and said she needed a coffee. She hasn't come back. How do I delete the post and make sure no one has read it?"

"It's too late for that. I took a look, and there are at least twenty responses already. I could delete the whole thing, but I don't know that it matters." Maybe a little come-to-Jesus with Dad wasn't such a bad idea.

Caroline's partner covered her mouth and bulged her eyes. "Oh, no—what have I done? I thought I was just…helping. She said she'd spent some time writing it and then I scared her and—"

Roger strode forward and hugged Abby. "Don't worry about it. Everything will be fine. Not too many people read your blog anyway. Besides, she needed to vent a little."

Abby reared back and searched his face. "You think so?"

He forced a reassuring smile that his insides hadn't supported. "I know so. Where'd she go?"

"She just left. I have no idea. You think she's seen it yet? Maybe not."

He hated to spoil her hopes, but there was no way in hell Caroline had missed all the responses. They'd automatically end up in her mail on her phone. There was enough male-bashing in those posts to start a gender revolution. "She's seen it, all right. The question is what will she do next? I need to find her."

Abby strummed her fingers on the store counter. "If she's seen them, she'll probably try to find her father and explain."

Of course she would. "Where does he live?"

"From what I understand, he's living in their cabin about an hour from here. I went with her ages ago when she first came back from her journalism job. I can draw you a map. It's a tough drive—not long, just rough."

It took Abby ten minutes to dictate her directions to Ben's cabin, and Roger patiently noted all her little remarks about where *not* to turn. Anyone else and he would have shut down all the superfluous information. He wasn't going to piss off Caroline's best friend when he needed her help.

• • •

Caroline turned her cell off after the fifteenth or so message chimed. If her father read all that crap, he'd be…hurt. Perhaps she should feel vindicated that he might get a nuance of the pain she'd endured all those years, but she didn't. He wasn't perfect and had been a complete absentee father, yet he was *here now*. Shouldn't that count for something? One thing she knew for certain: she didn't want him to leave again—at least not right away.

The road to the cabin was easy to miss. The simple dirt path that cut through the trees could easily be mistaken for a cattle trail, except for the gate and mailbox. She wondered how long it had been since that gate was closed. Vines had covered its rusted hinges and anchored it against the trees behind. Not much use for preventing access.

She bumped over the trail and stopped in front of the cabin. How long had it been since she'd seen the inside? Three years? No, five? She wasn't sure.

Caroline prayed her father didn't have any Internet access inside and hadn't used his phone. How many men his age actually used social media anyway? She'd just explain what happened, and they'd laugh it off and forget. The last thing she wanted was to piss him off and make him leave. Again.

She creaked the door on her vehicle shut and stepped carefully toward the door, avoiding roots and weeds. "Dad?"

Bam. The wind gushed from her stomach in one burst as she was body-slammed to the dust.

"Found you. Found you. Found you," a gleeful voice shouted against the back of her head. Huh? She wasn't exactly hiding. The taste of dirt filled her mouth and gritted against her teeth and lips. What the hell?

A heavy weight covered her body. She couldn't move—couldn't even see. Her face was crushed into the ground. This man accosting her was big, but boney and…shaking.

Caroline kicked her feet and tried to dislodge him. She gained a little ground and turned to get a glimpse.

The man continued to chant. *Found you, found you, found you.* Gray hair, blue eyes that glinted in a not-completely-*Deliverance* way, and a camouflage shirt. Hmmm. Okay, the shirt was a little scary, but otherwise he was just an old man. Of course, even old men could be dangerous. In fact, if she thought about it, a lot of criminals actually turned out to *be* old men.

What should she do? She was alone. Her father hadn't answered her call, and it was doubtful anyone else could hear her. She stared at the face for a couple beats. She had two choices, fight or surrender. Flight was out of the question with his bulk cementing her to the ground. The chanting grated; it was beyond annoying. She shoved her fear away and yelled, "STOP."

His craggy hands fell to his sides, and the man's eyes shuttered with calm. Like a child who had just been chastised for messing the kitchen while baking cookies for his mother, he pouted. In a hushed voice, he said the words once more. "Found you."

Had she hurt her captor's feelings? Seriously? Who cared? "Okay, okay—you found me. Now what?"

Her lungs were exploding from his weight on top of her. He appeared to be seventy if not older, his skin craggy from sun and age. He had her pinned, but the look on his face showed little triumph. Her skin crawled as the sticks underneath her poked and scratched. If he tried anything further, curled up his fists, or even hinted at a weapon—she was pretty confident she could take him.

His eyes fluttered. "Love me?"

"Pops, get off her. You'll crush the poor girl." Caroline swiveled her head, knowing a mass of twigs and leaves were lodged within her tresses. Finally, a voice she recognized. That was…

"Dad?"

"What brings you here in the middle of the day, sweetheart?" Her father seemed unconcerned with Rambo Senior straddling her midsection.

Oomph. Oomph. Her wind gushed as the man hopped on her stomach. Up. And. Down. With what little breath she had left, she shouted, "Can't. Breathe!"

"Pops, get off! I'm sorry, honey, it's a game he likes to play. It used to help him find his way home."

The order was heeded immediately, and Caroline sucked in as much air as she could. She rolled to her knees and lifted herself upright. Still on her knees, she peered at her father's shadow towering over them. "Mind introducing me to your kamikaze friend here first? Just in case I need to call the police or something. Or maybe an ambulance."

Bob shrugged. "Pops, this is Caroline."

The elderly man took her hand and pumped it almost as many times as he had chanted those monotonous words. She smiled weakly and worked her way back to full height. She twitched a leg in an attempt to remove the debris from her pants. Was that grass in her panties? Great. "Hi, Pops. Nice to meet you. What are you doing here? Are you a neighbor?"

Bob guffawed. "Not hardly. Come on, Caroline. You read my book, right? Look harder. Don't you recognize him?"

She plopped curled fists on hips in challenge. "Excuse me, but it's kind of hard to see when your eyes and nose are plastered in the dirt and you have a two-hundred pound chanting weight on your back." Caroline turned to the old man and pulled herself back into politeness mode. She did recognize him now: he was the old man at the art show the other night. "I'm Caroline. Your name, sir?"

He wiped his hand on his pants and rocked to his toes. "R—R—Rick." Clarity hit her like a brick. He was the man in her father's book—Patient R. A war hero and decorated veteran with no memory of his past. Her mouth fell open, and she bounced her eyes between the two men. "It's him? I mean—he's him? He's the patient you wrote about?"

Bob grinned in satisfaction. Was that because she actually *had* read the book, or something else? "Yep. There's more, too."

"You mean more than he likes to tackle complete strangers wherever he goes? Don't think for a minute I've forgotten about the dog pile at the art sale."

Her father bobbled his head like a ten-year-old with a secret. What could possibly top the fact that his father brought his research subject home? "He's your grandfather."

Chapter Twenty-Eight

Roger was skeptical as he bopped down the trail. It was rustic, remote, and bumpy as hell. He prayed he didn't tear up the bottom of his Land Rover. Was it a place to retreat or hide? Abby had referred to the area as a climber and hiker's paradise, and looking through the thicket of trees, it made sense. Periodically a trailhead opened, and he'd get a glimpse of the ruggedness surrounding the cabin he was sure to find—eventually.

He rolled down the windows and breathed in the earthy scent of the forest. Voices reached him over the sound of the engine's soft purr. Yelling. He surged forward and saw her car.

Then he saw her.

Caroline stood between her father and an older man, covered in dirt, leaves, and—was that a twig sticking out the back of her hair? What had happened?

Once he parked behind her car, he rushed to the group. She held out a hand to him, palm up. "I'm fine. So, grandfather? Really, Dad?"

Roger volleyed a look between the two. "Caroline, I saw—"

She lowered a brow and barked. "Haven't gotten to that part yet, because apparently Pops here is my *grandfather.* Did you know that? Am I the only one who was clueless?"

Roger watched the old man's face drain of color. Her expression could wilt a redwood. *Sucks to be you, old man.* "Nope, I wasn't aware either. Nice to meet you, sir."

The elderly gentleman responded eagerly to the handshake. His grip was solid but aggressive, and lingered more than was comfortable, pumping up and down repeatedly. "Nice to meet you."

Odd. Not scary, but odd in the way one sees when they know the person isn't necessarily as expected.

Introductions were made, and Bob ushered them all into the cabin. As Roger followed, he couldn't help but pick sticks and leaves from Caroline's hair and back. She shot him a frown, but he simply shrugged and continued. "You're kind of growing back there."

"You would be, too, if you'd been tackled by a two-hundred pound geriatric."

Bob didn't care for the insult. "Hey, watch it. You're talking about a decorated war veteran. Mind your tongue and be respectful."

The old man repeated, "Be respectful," as he shuffled behind them. It became obvious that he was strong, yet aged and somewhat handicapped. An *injured* war veteran perhaps?

Roger was more clueless than her apparently. At least *she* knew the man's story. "Really?"

Bob nodded. "Jacob Rickert, otherwise known as Patient R in my book, was lost after returning from Korea. My wife, Carol, had searched for him a few times, but it wasn't until she was diagnosed with her first bout of cancer that we really took it seriously. I spent two years over there trying to figure out what had happened to him, only to find out he was *here*. He had sustained a head injury and was shipped home, but his dog tags were misplaced during all the surgeries. We located records that showed he'd been discharged to a mental hospital four hours away.

"We were relieved and went to get him, but he'd recently escaped and no one had any idea where he was. My Carol was fit to be tied. Her dad, a war hero, wandering around in the streets alone with no one to care for him. We didn't sleep for days. She called every police station within five hours of the hospital. Oklahoma. Texas. She even called a couple in Louisiana, but the old bugger wasn't any less a hero with half his mental capacities. He walked his ass all the way from that mental hospital to this damned cabin in the woods. Can you believe that? The man can't remember a damn thing about his family or the war, but he found this house. *His* house."

Roger felt his mouth fall. "Wow, that's amazing. Was this his childhood home or something? I've heard sometimes we block out bad memories; maybe the war was too painful for him to remember."

Bob's eyes glittered. "Nope. I'd rather look at it a bit more romantically. He and his wife, my mother-in-law, lived here when first married. Actually, they didn't really live here—they spent their honeymoon here. It was all they could afford; it was free. She bought the place years later and held onto it all this time. We put a lot of great memories into this place since then, haven't we sweetheart?" He smiled Caroline's way.

She nodded. Roger took in the glassy sheen of her eyes. What do you know? She was finally speechless and not because she was angry.

Roger nodded. "Like I said, that's *amazing*." He patted Mr. Rickert on the back. "Well done, soldier."

The old man lifted a shaky hand and saluted Roger, then dropped into a chair by the window and watched the trees. He nodded and mumbled. "Yes, sir. Well done."

Caroline finally spoke. "So that's why you've stayed here since Mother died? You're taking care of him?"

Bob measured her words carefully before responding. "Honey, I left to do my job when you were a kid, and it kept me away. Your mom was strong, and we managed well enough for the short run. We always knew it was temporary. But when your mother was sick, I chucked it all and came home. She had to find him. I wanted to be here but knew it was important, too. For some reason, I know this is crazy, but I thought if I could find her father I'd save her. She'd somehow find the will or strength to fight off the disease."

Caroline put a hand to her hair and plucked another twig from the depths. "It was a disease of the body, not the heart."

"I know, but hell, a man will do anything to save his own heart." Bob followed Jacob's eyes to the trees.

Caroline played with the hem of her shirt. "You didn't answer my question."

Bob focused on her movements. "Yes, I'm taking care of him, but I *stayed* to be with my family."

"You mean him."

"No, I mean you, kid. Put that in your damn blog." His shoulders sagged.

As he watched this family reunion, Roger realized something that had never occurred to him before: Life's passions and purposes are insignificant without people around you to share them. People live and die for that one elusive need. He watched Caroline's face as she struggled to come to grip with her father's announcement, and his heart burned.

Chapter Twenty-Nine

Caroline drove home in a dust storm of confusion. She'd always envied what Roger had—a big family. Not necessarily *his* family, but any at all. Her mother had been the steady force in her life. She'd encouraged Caroline to go after her journalism career with gusto, and there'd never been an inkling of doubt that there'd be a home to visit should a problem arise.

Then she'd died, and all of Caroline's certainty evaporated in a few months. Her father had appeared from the outside edges of the earth, and now she had a grandfather who was a war hero with a disability? She sat in the car with the engine off and stared at her place, her fingers clutching the wheel. What a strange world.

Knock. Knock. Knock.

She turned and stared blindly through the glass. Roger? She rolled down the window. "You followed me home?"

He nodded, not one of those silly nods with his dimples in full bloom either. His eyes were filled with concern, wary of what she'd do or say. An incredible feeling of appreciation filled her— gladness that he was there. Not home or at work where he should be—but right there, staring at her and making her feel like she mattered. "Yeah, you've had a rough day, and I thought we might talk for a bit."

"I really don't want to discuss today."

He pulled on her door and wiggled his fingers for her to take them. "Neither do I—so let's talk photography. I have some pictures to show you."

"Of what? Some woman's toes or belly button?" She couldn't help but make at least one jab.

He half-grinned to acknowledge her bravado then sobered. "Nope, let's look at the ones from our park outing, okay?"

"You mean the day we nearly fell to our death from a tree?"

He shoved the door shut behind her and drew her fingers into his. "That's the one."

She wasn't really in the mood for company but looking at a bunch of pictures sounded harmless. Plus her curiosity wouldn't let her say no, so she shrugged and opened the door. "You should know I'm not the kind of person who likes to air dirty laundry, so don't expect me to spill my guts to you. Again."

He dropped her fingers and held up both hands. "No worries. I figure you spilled enough to the rest of the world on that blog of yours. You met your quota for the day. I might just hang around and watch the fallout, if that's all right."

Great. She rolled her shoulders and sighed. "This one's going to stay with me for a while, isn't it?"

He winked. "Probably. I can't speak for everyone else, but I'm willing to let it pass if you could give me a copy of Abby's screensaver at the store."

"Yeah, right, so you can post it on the Internet? Not happening, buddy."

"Don't worry. It would stay in my private stash."

She gave him a skeptical frown. "Right, like you did those beach shots from several years ago? Nah, I'll pass. Besides, it's not you I'm worried about—it's that creeper blog-guy that keeps harassing me."

"I could rough him up if you want. What's his name?" Inside, he cracked his knuckles and dropped onto the couch in a very non-threatening manner. Yeah, he was sooo intimidating.

"His name is Frederick, but I seriously doubt that's his real identity. He's been slamming me for ages on the blog, and I'm sure my latest post gave him great fodder for more abuse. I'm afraid to look. The only good part? Somehow our public arguing has been an advertising success. I guess people love to watch bloggers fight almost as much as they like watching boxers pummel each other into hamburger." In fact, she had half a mind to block the guy this time. In the past, the cat and mouse antics were fun, and it helped the store. Now? She wanted to spar with Frederick about as much as she wanted to eat chicken livers.

"Hmmm. He's probably eighty and thinks you're hot." Roger grabbed her remote and clicked on the flat screen. "I have the pictures on a flash drive. Can you load them on the screen, or should we use a computer?"

She clicked her fingers. "Hand it over—my laptop is synced to the screen."

He gave her the drive, and she plugged it into her laptop and double-clicked the first image. He could change the pictures with the remote, so she joined him on the couch. With her toes curled under a hip, she glanced at the screen and gasped. "Those are from that morning? Really?"

He grinned, and she couldn't help but take a quick look at the way his cheeks funneled around his mouth. "What do you think?"

"They're amazing! Look at the iridescence of the water shining through the leaves." She pointed at the screen but knew he'd already seen it—hell, he'd done the work. He flicked through a few more photos, and Caroline had a thought. "We could sell these in our shop, you know. You could enlarge them, and we could sell them. Because of your success at the fundraiser, we could even bill you as a local artist, and you'd make a mint. They'd sell like crazy."

He put the remote down and turned to meet her gaze. "That's not why I'm showing you." The look on his face was apprehensive. Oh, hell, now what? What else could possibly happen today? She waited for him to speak. "Do you remember that tree, Caro? It was huge, and the limbs were ratty and worn."

She nodded. "It looked half-dead to me."

"We made it look like heaven in these pictures. Like a palm tree in the middle of the desert."

She shook her head because she had nothing to do with the photos. "Not me. You did."

"You were there with me. I would have never seen the opportunity had it not been for you."

She seriously doubted it but wasn't going to argue. He was leading her somewhere, and she was in no mood to resist. The day had been too long and tiring. "Okay, I was *there*. That's all—you did all the work. Other than holding the camera equipment, I had nothing to do with your vision. How was I supposed to know you planned to do that?"

He pointed a finger her way, lifted his thumb, and gave a quick trigger action. "Bingo."

"What do you mean?"

He stood, placed his arms beside her on the couch, and leaned in, giving her a wonderful whiff of his cologne. Wow, that Polo is one potent scent when it can overpower the grime she was encrusted in from her earlier tumble. He kissed her forehead and whispered, "Think about it. I'll see you tomorrow."

He padded out the door and left her with the pictures and another puzzle.

•••

At home, Roger let Conan out to water his normal spots and dropped to his favorite place on the steps. Taking advantage of the wait, he dialed his mother, his oldest sister, then Carter. Once he'd divulged his plans, he retrieved his laptop and read Caroline's blog post again. He let out a couple laughs and thought for a few minutes before starting to type. Hell, if she was going to drop such a bomb on the world, he might as well join the ruckus. He only hoped she wouldn't have a heart attack. Or shoot him.

Chapter Thirty

Caroline stared at the picture on her flat screen for another five to ten minutes after Roger dropped his riddle in her lap. The display held fifty inches of red, green, and brown with a smidge of yellow and two bright white dots glaring at her like—boobs. Oh. My. God. The leaves surrounded the pinpoints of light in perfect full-blossomed beauty. Had he intended such a curvaceous reference?

The leaves were…voluptuous. She burst into laughter. Heat rose from her chest into her face. She laughed until tears surged into her eyelashes, and she blinked rapidly in an attempt to contain the hysteria. What would *that* picture sell for at the next fundraiser? How on earth had he managed to make something so ordinary become sensual?

She switched the flat screen off and wondered…was that what he wanted her to notice? His puzzle? The man was hopeless. She shook her head and retreated to bed without viewing the remaining photos.

At work the following morning, Abby was quiet for the first hour, which amazed Caroline. She'd fully expected to be interrogated or chastised for running off, but nothing happened. The room was so full of silence it felt like outer space. When Abby finally opened her mouth to speak, Caroline felt a gush of relief flow from her chest. "You okay, friend?"

"Yeah, sorry I ditched you yesterday. I was a brat."

Abby was concentrated on an arrangement for an upcoming wedding. Biting her lip with both hands working the ribbon around a bouquet, she shook her head. "Nothing compared to what I've done with the texting mess. Don't worry about it. This too shall pass."

Caroline doubted that, but nodded and grabbed a watering tin to begin reviving the plants on the floor. There was something rejuvenating about their little endeavor. Every morning she walked in and inhaled a deep breath of roses, carnations, lavender, and all the other fantastic smells. It was comforting and yes, rejuvenating.

Abby finished the bouquet, added it to a box, then began the next. "Besides, your little rant was nothing compared to all the crap our followers wrote. I wonder if we'll see a barrage of customers today—people whose curiosity got the best of them and who want check out the local pariah."

Great. "A bunch of busybodies wandering around watching me as if I'll eventually lose it and go on a rage—I could have fun with that, you know."

Abby chuckled. "As long as you don't chase off any of our hard-earned and *paying* customers, go for it. Just warn me so I can film the whole thing. I'll be right back. I want to go enter our receipts from yesterday into the computer. You okay here?"

Caroline darted a glance around the empty store. "Does it look like I'm swamped?"

Ignoring her sarcasm, Abby disappeared to the back office. She hadn't asked how things went with her father. Nor had she hovered, expecting her to break down at any moment. She'd only shown concern for her well-being.

Caroline appreciated her nonjudgmental acceptance. Cars buzzed by on the street outside, many of them police cars in the process of a shift change. Overhead, soft rock oozed from the speakers. Their little shop felt more like home than her tiny two-bedroom. It also felt…empty. And too damn quiet.

"Hey, did I tell you I have a family?" She shouted the words toward the back. "It's so crazy, but I chased my dad down—and guess what? Not only has he waltzed back into my life after years, but now, on top of *that* drama, I have a grandfather living with him. He's old and somewhat handicapped—and a decorated war hero. He's also prone to wandering away. Can you believe that?" Her words echoed in the empty room.

The door to the office creaked. Abby stepped forward, crossed her arms, and leaned against the doorjamb. "How do you feel about that?"

Caroline stopped watering and met her gaze. "You sound like a shrink. How do I feel about it? Confused. Angry. Disbelieving. I don't know—pissed off more than anything. Why the hell did they not tell me all this earlier?"

Abby dropped her hands and walked to Caroline's side. "Who knows, but does it matter? You know now. Question is, what're you gonna do?" Abby rubbed a warm hand up Caroline's arm and squeezed her shoulder. "You should go take a look at the computer. I was reading the blog a second ago, and—"

Caroline put the watering can down. "I know. I know. I accidentally posted something I shouldn't have. I'm sorry. It was an accident."

"No, I hit the post button. I thought you were ready and hadn't even read the words, but that's not what I was talking about— there's more."

Caroline started toward the back. "I saw the responses. Why don't I take the post down? That way we won't get any additional bad publicity."

"Just read the responses. They're not all bad. Then do whatever you feel is best."

That was cryptic. A few seconds later, Caroline stared at the computer screen. She drew a hand over her mouth and reread the next-to-last post—from her buddy Frederick.

Hey, gorgeous. How dare he start like that?

Regarding the daisies: They're perfect, and if you like what I'm about to say, I'll give them to you at least once a week—can't promise every day.

Uh-oh, that sounded a little creepy.

Regarding your dad, we can't pick our family, but we can either choose to love them or not—love them or leave them, so to speak. He came back into your life for a reason, and that reason could only mean that he felt he needed to be with you and know you. That's a gift.

Regarding do-overs, a few years ago a woman I adored left me to pursue a dream that was important to her. Recently I found her again, and I've debated how to handle the situation. She's annoyed me, angered me, humored me, and made my heart split in two. But the one thing I know with certainty, now that the years have passed, is that being with her and experiencing all those crazy emotions fills a void in my life. I NEED her more than I need to breathe.

Lastly, some may think me an eighty-year-old grumpmeister with nothing better to do than pester a young shop owner. Deduct fifty years from that, and you'd be right—I have nothing better to do because that shop owner, a petite little brunette in crazy clothes and crazy hair, is the woman I need. The woman who left me years ago.

Caroline, it's me, Roger. I'm crazy about you.

Her mouth popped open. "Are you fricking kidding me? Frederick is *Roger?*"

"Yeah, isn't that sweet?" Abby popped up beside her.

"No. It's not. It's a mean, mean prank. Stupid. Selfish. That self-absorbed, self-righteous, uh, *asshole.*" Caroline felt the hair on her neck bristle.

"You're the one being stupid now. The man just bared his soul—publicly, might I remind you—and expressed his feelings for you to the entire world. That may be a little crazy and risky, but it's definitely sweet and very, very romantic."

Caroline rested her hands on the keyboard and tapped her leg up and down. What should she do?

Abby grabbed her wrists and focused on Caroline's face. "Don't you dare thrash him on that blog, you hear me? If you have a problem, you get your ass out there and face it. Don't be a coward and send off a rant that's shielded between layers of technology."

Caroline lifted a brow. "Seriously? This is coming from *you*? The woman who carried on weeks and weeks of texting deception?"

Abby released her wrists with a mean little shove. "That's exactly why I said that—face him and talk. In person."

"We're *working*." She reminded.

Abby whirled the chair around and pulled Caroline from the cushion. "No, *I'm* working—you're officially off for the day. Move it."

"But I was gone yesterday."

Abby shooed her away. "Get going. I'm a big girl. I can handle this."

Chapter Thirty-One

When Caroline arrived at Roger's office, the receptionist gave her a puzzled look. "It's not Tuesday."

"I'm not here for the plants. I'm here to kick someone's ass." Caroline stomped past and strode to Roger's door. Without knocking, she shoved her way inside and slammed it shut.

Roger blinked and reared back in his seat. "Heyyy, there."

"Don't *hey there* me, buddy. Where do you get off putting all that stuff on our blog and pestering me for weeks and weeks?"

A cough startled her, and Caroline whirled to see Carter. "Oh, hi. You should probably leave—this is going to get ugly."

Carter needed no further prompting. He bolted out the door, leaving it wide open. Roger stood, rounded his desk, and eased it shut before leaning forward—right into her. "How ugly?"

She raised an index finger and poked his chest. "You. Have. No. Idea. What the hell, Roger? You've been harassing me all this time? Baiting me and criticizing and—"

"I wasn't criticizing."

"Oh no, you were just debating every comment or analogy I wrote. Don't you have anything better to do?"

He backed her against the doorframe and anchored himself by placing his palms on the door, one on each side of her face. "No, actually I don't. Did you read what I said, Caro?"

"What *you* said? Or what *Frederick* said? And where did you get such a stupid alias anyway? Couldn't you have picked something normal like *Anonymous* or *Bob*?"

"Frederick was the last name of a guy I knew. Conan was his first name."

"Oh. So, you're blogging as a dog."

Roger shot his eyes toward the ceiling then leaned closer and moved his palms to her cheeks, holding her hostage with his hands and body. She should wriggle free, or push him away, but the urge to do so wavered. Then it disintegrated. God help her, but she loved the feel of him melded against her. Her body betrayed her by moving her legs open so he could nestle closer. "The name doesn't matter, honey. Did you read the words? I meant them. I need you in my life, Caroline Sanders. Every crazy, mean, funny, beautiful inch of you. Did you get that?"

She felt the steady bump, bump, bump of his heart pressed against her chest and his legs strong and solid between her own. Her stomach clenched, prompting her to answer. "Yeah, I got that." She had no idea what to say next.

"Good." He leaned in and kissed her, soft and loving pecks that deepened into wet, hard kisses that made her want to undress him. When he finally stepped back and gave her air, her fingers were inside his shirt, circling the little hairs around his navel. His shirt hung loose from his pants.

"So what does that mean?"

He shrugged. "Whatever you want it to. I told you how I feel—no, I told the entire Internet how I feel. I need you in my life. That's pretty much it. The rest is up to you."

Up to her. Well, that made her feel incredibly *in control.* "Okay, then."

Roger coughed. "Except." He paused.

Caroline wrapped her arms over his shoulder and clasped her fingers together. "Except what? Whatever it is, we're not doing it here."

He grinned, a full dimpled heart-stopping grin. "I like the way your mind works, but I was going a little deeper. I need you in my life, and I mean that. But I'm not going to lie. I want *all* of you, Caro. I even want the piece you left over there in a little town called Teslehad on the other side of the world."

She swallowed. "What are you saying?"

He thumbed her cheeks. "You have to go back over there and get that piece back, honey. You'll never get past it until you face it."

What? "Oh, hell no. I am definitely *not* doing that again."

She shoved against his chest. Roger's words echoed through her head, but she ignored them—in fact, all she heard was a thundering roar. Of gunfire and children's voices. She slammed her hands over her ears. "No. No. No."

Caroline flung the door open and raced to the elevator, and Roger followed her inside. He held her arms, but she pulled away. He groaned. "Come on, Caroline. You know it has to happen. You'll never get past it and be yourself if you don't go back."

Chapter Thirty-Two

Caroline watched the rearview mirror, barely registering the road ahead. His silhouette, standing at the curb, gradually receded as the knot in her stomach grew. How could he possibly ask her to give up everything she'd worked for to go back there?

She'd finally attained some stability in her life, and he wanted her to throw it away? It was crazy. It was irresponsible. It was… tempting.

No. Scratch that idea—it was *crazy*. Yep, dumbest idea ever. Caroline turned her concentration to the road. She pressed the gas, feeling the engine kick, and noted the intersection ahead. Where should she go?

Glancing at her choices, each of them took her farther from Roger and away from potential drama. That was good, right? The car rolled to a reluctant stop, and the engine idled in bursts. She searched the rearview mirror for images of his building, but bushes, trees, and cars swallowed her view. Perhaps the chugging engine was prodding her to stop.

Caroline thrust the car in park and pressed her forehead to the steering wheel. *He needed me.* What was that supposed to mean? She had no idea. She'd never needed anyone in her life, except her mother—and she'd left. Hell, everyone in her life had left her at some point. Her father, Roger, and every man she'd ever dated since. Okay, technically she'd left Roger before he had the chance, and her mother hadn't left—she'd *died*, but that was still leaving, wasn't it?

That was what people did. They left. They moved on with their lives, leaving her with the painful burden of their absence.

The horn of a car behind her honked. Still unsure where to go, she pulled forward and looped into a parking spot. Once the other vehicle had passed, she started driving back down the street.

He needed me—no, that's not how he said it. He said he needs me. Now, not then. Would he still feel that way in a month?

Wait. She flipped the rearview mirror to check her eyes and wipe away the water that puddled and smeared her makeup. Reality check, woman. What he needed wasn't the issue. Nor did it matter what he'd feel in a month or a year.

The tires crunched on broken concrete as her car rolled toward his building. Roger sat on a bench, his hands draped over his knees and head bent. He lifted his head and met her eyes through the windshield.

Caroline drank him in, swallowed her fear, and stepped from the car. Another horn honked as a car whizzed by, nearly grazing her hip.

Time stood still. "What's wrong? You forget something?" There was a glint of hope in his chocolate eyes.

She focused on that and moved toward him, then plopped to his side on the bench. "No, I wanted to say something."

He stared at his feet. "Caro. Let's not draw this out—at least when you left before, there was a note. It was done. You didn't have to say goodbye. The only thing I had trouble with was the fact that you had no problem leaving, that I didn't matter. Now, you leave again, and—"

"Stop talking, please. It wasn't that you didn't matter. Back then, I had to go—you know that. Don't you remember what you said? People need three things in life, the most important of which is a passion—a purpose."

Finally, he lifted his eyes and focused on her. "I said that?"

She nodded. "But you were wrong. Yeah, I know, amazing—don't snicker."

"I wasn't snickering."

"You snickered. Like it or not, you've turned into a good guy, Roger. Don't get all excited about it…and don't think you'll always be right, because you won't. The third thing isn't a purpose or passion. The purpose I can live without. I got all the way down to the end of the street and sat there. For the life of me, I had no idea where I was going. I knew where I lived, where I worked, where I thought I belonged. But I had a huge problem with *leaving you.* I'd already done it once and I…just…couldn't. Then I realized why. I don't really *need* to go fricking find myself."

They focused on each other's faces, and she saw moisture in his eyes. That was new. He blinked. "Okkaay."

"So, here's the deal. I *need* you, too. Sure, I love you, but that's not the problem." He cocked a hopeful brow, and she saw a flicker of movement in the dimples. She stroked a finger along the lines of his face.

"Does that mean you're going over there and then coming back to me?" He shuffled his legs around and slid a knee behind her on the bench.

"It means you're wrong."

He frowned.

"That third thing that people must have in life is to be loved—and needed."

He nodded and pulled her in tight. He lifted her legs over his then wrapped her in a hug. For the first time *ever*, she knew exactly where her place in life was—and is.

"Okay, this time, I guess I can be wrong. I love you, Caroline."

She lifted both hands to his cheeks and moved to touch their noses together. "I love you too. Isn't it cool?"

His shoulders moved a tad, and his dimples twitched as if afraid to show themselves. "But…"

Uh oh. There was more? "But what?"

"But let's not completely rule out that passion thing, okay?"

"What do you mean?"

"It means you were meant to be a journalist, gorgeous. You have to go back over there and write the real story."

What the hell was he talking about? She *had* written the story. It was horrible—and she knew because the nightmares reminded her constantly. "I am never going back."

He put his thick, warm fingers over hers. "You are—and I'm going with you. You're going to write a different story. I'll be right there. We'll give those kids a proper ending to show their lives mattered. To show who loved and *needed* them."

She shuddered. "No."

"Yes."

"It's over."

He tapped her forehead. "Not up here, it isn't."

She opened her mouth to argue, but he brought the fingers down to her lips. She stopped.

"Caro, you need the happy ending. For all your strength and toughness, that's your thing. People love it, too—it's inspiring. Hell, who doesn't want the fairytale? Let's go over there and get one. You and me. Damn everything else to hell. We deserve ours, and you're going to write about it—our happy ending. Theirs, too."

"Your family needs you."

"I've been here for them most of my life. They can take care of themselves for a change. Let's focus on that third thing—let's focus on *us*. Okay?" He bent to kiss her, gentle and soft, and gave her a squeeze.

Us. She'd never been part of any *us* before—she liked the way it rolled off his tongue. She liked the warm cozy way it felt. She nodded and wrapped her arms around his neck. "Us. Yes. Definitely okay."

About the Author

Shelley K. Wall was born near Kansas City, the middle daughter of three. She is a graduate of Oklahoma State University with additional postgraduate work there and at the University of Wyoming extension in Casper. She worked for many years in Information Technologies as a Network Engineer, a Project Manager, Operations Director, and I.T. Department Head. In addition to her writing efforts, she continues to maintain her technical certifications in various technologies and consults regularly on projects. After writing numerous Project Plans, I.T. Directives, Budgets, Personnel Evaluations, and Strategic Plans, she found fiction to be thoroughly refreshing and a wonderful creative outlet.

She is a member of Romance Writers of America,Sisters In Crime (SinC), the Houston Literary Guild, and various technical organizations.She writes daily and speaks on subjects pertaining to authorship and fiction writing.

Her first release, *Numbers Never Lie*, debuted in 2012 and was an Amazon Daily Deal in January. It soared to number three for romantic suspense, eight for contemporary romance, and seventeen in overall romance on the Amazon Bestsellers List. She has since written over a dozen more novels of contemporary romance or romantic suspense.

Website: *http://shelleykwall.com*
Blog: *http://shelleykwall.wordpress.com*
Twitter: @skwallbooks

More from This Author
(From *Find Me* by Shelley K. Wall)

Amanda Gillespie wasn't about to let the bile in her stomach keep her from showing up at the damn outdoor adventure club meeting. It was just nerves. She could do this. *Had* to do this, since she'd stupidly, irresponsibly taken her friend Darlene's bet that she wouldn't. Now five hundred bucks hung in the balance.

She smoothed her skirt and shoved through the door of the beautiful eighty-story Darshwin Tower, wishing she'd gone home to change clothes after work. But that would have made her late to the meeting, and there was no way in hell Darlene was going to give her peace if that happened.

Darlene Fitch was a bulldog both in reputation and stature. Though small, her mind was a flytrap of details that made her one of the best criminal attorneys in the state of Texas. Amanda strived to be half as good. Darlene had a ten-year start on her, so maybe in time she'd get there. The woman was also faultlessly protective of her friends—not in a motherly way, but in an in-your-face, don't-fuck-with-my-friend way.

Why Darlene had turned Amanda into a pet project was a mystery.

"You're such a workaholic pansy. Just enjoy yourself—have fun for a change," Darlene had tossed at her after they'd finished eating lunch over legal briefs a week earlier.

"I am *not*. I have fun."

"Really? Prove it. When's the last time you did anything that didn't have a roof and an air conditioner involved? Or traded those heels for a pair of sneakers, for that matter?"

Amanda sighed. "Okay, so maybe I prefer to be clean and… and I have allergies."

Darlene rolled her eyes. "Oh, brother. To what? A good time? Amanda Gillespie, we're going to get your blood pumping if it kills us. Or maybe just you. I'm too young to die. Besides, how are you ever going to date someone who doesn't have their nose in legal briefs if you don't leave the office?"

"Maybe I like briefs."

Darlene giggled. "I like briefs too—or boxers—or nothing at all. They're all good. Listen, we all know you can kick ass as a lawyer but can you do it outside in the fresh air? I highly doubt it. I think you're a born and bred book-addicted *nerd*."

That was the challenge that took her over the top. Competitiveness was bred deep in the Gillespie family and challenges of any sort rarely went unanswered. That was what happened when you grew up in a household with two older brothers. Everything was a contest. Amanda took the bait, and agreed to Darlene's bet proposal: Whoever did better on two out of the three challenges would win. Now she was regretting it.

Amanda clip-clopped on high heels toward the elevator bank and her cell phone rang. She glanced at the display, then snapped it to her ear. "What? You're checking up on me? I'm at the elevator, Give me five minutes."

Darlene laughed. "Cluck, cluck, cluck, cluck …"

Is she really insinuating I'm chicken? "Oh, stop. I'll be there before you can find your next client."

Sure, it was a jab to mention Darlene's ambulance chasing but the woman actually admitted to perusing the daily paper for victims. Er, clients. Amanda strung the strap of her briefcase over her shoulder and sandwiched the phone above it between her ear and the shoulder pad of her suit. With her other hand, she unknotted her scarf, slipped two buttons of her silk shirt open, and let out a sigh. "You could have picked something a little closer to the office, you know. I had to practically jog in these damned heels. I think I have a blister."

"You should carry loafers like I do. Hurry up. The instructor is tall, tanned, and tight-ass free, something we rarely meet…uh, oh. I think he heard me. Gotta go."

Amanda grinned as the phone went silent. For a woman with a stellar legal career, Darlene despised attorneys—a.k.a. tight-asses—and had a strict rule about dating them. The irony of her choosing not to date someone of her own species apparently escaped her brilliant brain. But, based on the few single attorneys Amanda knew, Darlene wasn't all wrong.

Amanda punched the elevator button and stepped into the first one that opened. Five hundred bucks was a lot of money, and she planned to win. Neither of the women was athletic, but Amanda was pretty sure she could handle herself well enough to best her friend. Betting she could beat Darlene in a couple of outdoor activities seemed an easy win.

• • •

For Jackson Holstenar, the elevator was a fundamental part of life. It was how he traveled to the gym on the top floor of the building, to his friend Carter's office, to his father's office, to his own office. Though his berth could hardly be called an office. His choice. His father wanted him upstairs with the bigwigs, but Jackson preferred to pay his dues like all the other new staff.

He waited for the doors to open. Carter had wanted to talk about his new project before the weekend adventure seekers group. Ever since Jackson had accidently gotten Carter fired, he felt guilty and listened patiently to Carter's work stories. The firing had been unintentional—Jackson had mouthed off at a project manager because he and their friend Roger wanted to set them up. She hadn't liked the comments and blew a gasket before complaining to Carter's management team. Carter had taken the heat because

Jackson's dad just ignored the complaint. Carter's new job seemed to fit better, so it wasn't a complete loss.

Jackson's phone signaled a text message from Carter. *Let's just talk after the group meeting. I'm already there.*

Ding.

The doors slipped open. He smelled oranges. *That* brought back memories. He glanced over at the tall blonde with her hair sleeked into a gold barrette. Was he hallucinating? It had been eighteen months since he'd seen Amanda Gillespie. He stuck an arm out as the doors started closing, then stepped into the elevator. No, it was her.

Could he really have missed her annoying perfume?

"Amanda?"

The woman in the peach twill suit stopped fumbling with her bag and popped her head up, her sea-blue eyes widening like portholes on a Caribbean cruise ship.

"Oh my God. Jackson! What are you doing here?"

His throat threatened to choke back his words and he swallowed. "I'm meeting a friend in a few minutes upstairs. What about you?"

Amanda slicked a hand over her hair. "Me too. Sort of. I'm a little late actually. Work. You know."

Was that supposed to mean he knew how harried her new job was? He didn't. Not anymore. Not since she'd quit working at his dad's office and sneaked out without even saying goodbye.

He still felt the sting. "Work. Of course."

Jackson focused on the lit elevator panel and the soft sounds as they moved higher. The seconds it took to rise to his floor seemed like hours. A thousand questions fogged his brain but he wouldn't ask any of them. Nope. She'd run out without telling a soul because that was what she wanted. No explanation. No apology. And no indication of where she'd be in the future. She ran *away*. From their work relationship and their friendship. Hell—she'd fallen off the planet.

Jackson sure as hell wasn't going to ask why. Not now. When the doors opened, he motioned for her to lead and followed her down the hall—to the same door he sought. Should he turn around and leave? Admittedly, seeing her brought mixed emotions—shitty and relieved ones. Did he really want to deal with that? He couldn't abandon Carter. They'd been friends forever and hadn't seen each other in a while.

"You're going here too?" Amanda frowned. Apparently she wasn't all that excited about seeing him either.

He nodded. "I had no idea you were into this kind of thing." The only athletic thing he'd seen her do was jog and that was only one time when she'd been trying to catch a bus. Still, based on the muscle tone in her legs, she didn't spend all her time on a sofa.

"I'm not. My friend Darlene bet me five hundred bucks that I couldn't do at least two of the three challenges better than she did. Apparently I don't have an adventurous bone in my body. But since neither of us has done anything like this, I figured my size would give me an advantage. I'm five inches taller and have not only the height advantage but longer legs."

Inside the room, voices tumbled excitedly over the wild beat of some sort of retro music. Jackson couldn't place the band but he felt the energy.

"Hey! There you are." Carter rushed forward and circled an arm over Jackson's shoulder, then scooped Amanda in as well. What the hell?

Carter kissed her on the cheek and Jackson could tell he'd had a beer before showing up, maybe two. He was relaxed. Loose. Not his normal tight-wound demeanor. "So, this is your new girlfriend, Jax? Wow. She's gorgeous."

Amanda pulled free and frowned. "Um, hell no, I'm not with *him*. I'm with *them*." She pointed across the room where two women beckoned for her to join. "Good luck with that new girlfriend, *Jax*." Amanda's tight business skirt snapped as she clipped away.

Carter coughed. "Wow, should have known you'd never score a chick like that. What was I thinking? So, where is the new love?"

Jackson shrugged. "Gone. We stopped dating a couple weeks ago. She wanted serious and I wanted anything but. So, what d'ya think about this shindig?" The two men strode to the nearest chairs and plopped down. It felt good to sit and stretch a bit.

The instructor, who called himself a *coordinator*, introduced the other organizers and outlined their first three outings. All three were mild for Jackson's taste: a hike through the canyon near Fredericksburg, zip lining above the trees near the lake, and a mud run obstacle course. Easy-peasy.

Jackson was tired and figured he'd listened attentively enough so he searched the room. For Amanda.

"Introduce me."

"What?" Jackson returned his thoughts to Carter and the group surrounding him.

"Introduce me to that girl you came in with. You obviously know her."

"She came up the elevator with me."

"Yeah, saw that…but you know her, right?"

"Sort of. She used to work with me. She left a year and a half ago."

"Good, then you'll make a great wing man. Let's go." Carter yanked Jackson's sleeve and slid from his chair.

Jackson cringed. "You really don't want to know this one, Carter. She's…high maintenance."

Carter punched Jackson's arm. "She can't be all bad if she showed up for this club. You're the one who said I should get out there and meet someone. Besides, I had a great week. I'm on a roll. This might be good."

Yeah, but roll somewhere else, man. Not toward her. Jackson pushed out of his cushy comfortable chair. Perfect. He was introducing his best friend to the one girl who was off limits—for him, and everyone else. She kept everyone in the "friendship" category, which was where she'd shoved him years ago when they were classmates.

As they strode toward the women, Amanda met his gaze. Jackson held onto her eyes like they were liquid gold. How should he do this? Her friend swiveled to look over her shoulder and gasped. "Well, aren't you a tall thing? You look like you could shimmy through that obstacle course like nobody's business and come out slathered with mud in all the right places."

Jackson blinked. Her friend was giving him the once-over. "And I bet you'd make mud-wrestling an art form. This is Carter Coben." He waved a hand at his best friend who completely honed in on Amanda. "And I'm Jackson." He offered a hand to the shorter woman.

"Darlene. And this is Amanda." The two were as opposite as night and day and appeared significantly different in age as well. Amanda had to be significantly younger. How'd they ever become friends? "We're attorneys over at—"

Oh, of course. Darlene the Bulldog. He'd seen her ads. "I recognize you now, though you should sue your marketing group. Those ads don't do you justice."

Darlene giggled and put a hand to her throat. Jackson let the smile on his face go dead as Carter wedged between them and sat next to Amanda. Carter put a hand on his leg and flexed his bicep, his signature move. Jackson rolled his eyes.

"You ladies like to do these things a lot?" Carter asked.

Carter had made one small error in his move: He'd left a comfortable amount of personal space between himself and Amanda. Jackson flopped down between them and threw his arms behind their chairs. "Don't kid yourself, Carter. Amanda here won't even step in a rain puddle, let alone do a mud run. And I'd bet the only thing she's climbed or hiked lately is the Galleria Mall when there's a shoe sale. Right, Mandy?"

Jackson noticed her pink cheeks and the flash of fire that swept through her baby-blues. She clucked and tapped a palm to his face. "Oh, Jax. It's so nice to see you throwing your typical childish bullshit insults again. Don't you think you're a little old for that?"

Darlene's mouth dropped. "You guys know each other?"

Amanda huffed. "No."

It came in unison with Jackson's "Yes." He grinned.

"Figures," Darlene said. "I'm always late to the party."

Amanda sighed. "Jackson's an attorney, too. We worked together very briefly."

Jackson cocked his head sideways. "Yes, *briefly.* Why is that, Amanda? Why so briefly?"

The crowd had begun to disperse as people signed up for whatever events they chose then gathered belongings and left. Amanda stood and thumbed at the lists, ignoring his jab. "Gotta go, gentlemen. I have money to win and work to get back to. Nice meeting you, Carter." She waved, then cast a hate glare Jackson's way before striding off. Her friend Darlene followed after tossing him a quick wink.

Carter frowned. "That went well. You could have at least tried to be civil long enough to give me a shot."

Jackson shrugged and pointed at the wall of paper with scribbled names. "You don't need my help. This one's a no-brainer. Go look at what she's signed up for and put your name on the same list."

Revelation crossed his features. "Think I will."

Once Carter left, Jackson followed his own advice and added his name to the lists as well. No sense in letting Carter get kicked around without his wing man.

The following Sunday afternoon, Jackson stood by his Jeep, sipping cold coffee and watching Amanda's tight shorts rise up her ass while she lifted gear from the back of an SUV. Great way to start the day. He leaned against the hood, crossed his legs, and took another sip. "Need some help with that?"

She lowered the box onto the ground and glared at him. *Hmmm. Nice to see you too.* She tossed her hair back and returned to digging through the trunk.

Jackson tossed the paper cup in the trash bin beside his car, then strode her way. "Guess you didn't hear me. Do you—"

"I heard you. I just didn't answer. If I needed help, I'd ask for it. Okay?"

Carter shoved in front, scooped the box from the dirt, and pulled a bag from her hands. "What kind of guy lets a woman carry heavy boxes while he's empty handed? Come on, the group's already starting toward the trailhead. Are you planning to take all of this on the hike?"

Amanda opened her mouth to protest, then stopped. She gave Carter one of those dazzling smiles and Jackson cringed. He remembered how many times she'd used that look with him. It had caught his breath on occasion but he shrugged it off as hormones—or maybe just hadn't understood. Carter stopped for a second. Yep, that look went straight to the man parts and his friend wasn't immune, damn him. It wasn't jealousy seething through Jackson's skin. Amanda was like a sister. Okay, she *had* kissed him a little too passionately one night in law school when they were both drunk. *That* had stunned him, coming from her. Still, she deserved better and he'd managed to keep the losers away before. But Carter? He wasn't a loser. So why the hell did the fact that it was Carter bother him more? "That's sweet of you. No, I just wanted to put the drinks in the coolers for the after-party.

John, the organizer, said we could drop them off at the starting point. Do you mind carrying them that far?"

Carter winked and threw the box onto his shoulder. "Piece of cake. You look amazing, by the way."

Amanda slammed her trunk closed and dropped a hand into the pocket of her tight cargo shorts. She shot Carter another megawatt smile. "Thanks. I wasn't really sure what was appropriate for this kind of thing."

Jackson felt his face flush. Seriously? She was flirting?

Steam started to rise from his already sweating forehead. Couldn't she see what an idiot/asshole Carter was? Surely Jackson wasn't the only person to notice his complete lack of personality. Sure, they were best friends but friends know each other's faults best.

Amanda tucked a hand into Carter's arm and walked alongside as he toted her things.

At the trail head, the organizer handed out maps to everyone, then told them to be back at five. "The sun goes down at six so if we don't have a full headcount at five fifteen, we'll send out a search party." The man laughed, then waved his hands like Moses sending his flock into the ship, two by two. Carter dropped into step by Amanda and her friend. It was a dumb move since the path wasn't wide enough. Then Jackson had a thought.

He and Carter had competed in almost everything since they were kids. Technically it started right after Carter's sister died but he never brought up specific dates. Carter was strong and built like a college quarterback. He worked hard to stay fit and hated that Jackson's natural athleticism often beat out his own work ethic. Jackson sidled up to his friend. "Have you looked at the map yet?"

Carter glinted into the sun above Jackson's head. "No, why?"

Jackson unfolded the paper. "There are four trails. Each one is different and they're classified by difficulty. Let's take this one here and first one to the summit buys the other a beer."

Carter glanced at the map. "You do realize that the drinks in the cooler are free and they have beer, water, and juices? Technically, we're not buying anything."

Jackson slapped Carter on the back. "Such a smart ass. Okay, then first one up to the summit and back wins. That means the first to reach that cooler full of drinks."

Carter's eyes flickered with interest. "What do I win?"

"Assuming you actually make it down first, you win…I don't know. What about …"

Amanda twisted the cap off a water bottle with a click. "Skinny dipping in the river behind those trees while the rest of us cook and clean up."

Gulp. Jackson leaned into her ear and whispered, "Would that be with or without you?"

Her hair whipped his cheek as she stepped into a power walk. She glanced over her shoulder. "Without. This isn't a team event. See you in my dust, Jax."

Hmm. That idea backfired. Beating Carter would be easy; the guy never bested him at anything. Beating Amanda, though? He could do it but she might hate him even more.

Four more steps and she vanished into the trees. The image of Amanda skinny dipping stopped him dead for a couple of seconds. Long enough for Carter to dart past and disappear behind her. Oh, hell no. If anyone was going to be in that ice-cold, fish-infested water with—or just watching—Amanda, it wasn't going to be Carter.

Jackson took off at a trot. It took him about five minutes to catch Carter. He yanked him by the neck and shoved him into the trees before focusing on the back pockets of Amanda's shorts. Thank God she hadn't seen his strong-arming. Carter rustled out of the undergrowth. "Hey, asshole. You're dead meat."

Jackson picked up his pace. Amanda was about fifteen yards ahead. Unfortunately, the path tilted upward. Her calves tightened and bulged as she stair-stepped up and over rocks. Jackson followed suit. Long legs were a distinct advantage when it came to rugged terrain. Within minutes, he was behind Amanda. He glanced upward at the rocks and pine needles, seeking a solid footing so he could make his move. He dug into the pebbled dirt with his toes and lunged forward.

A vise grip clamped around his ankle and killed his forward movement. What the hell? Jackson teetered and fell to a knee. Below him Carter cursed and held tight to his other leg. Jackson kicked. "Let go before we both roll down the hill."

"Nope. You're going down."

"Like hell." Jackson kicked again. The movement caused him to lose his footing. He hit the dirt like a sack of potatoes, mashing his face into the side of the rock-covered hill, and his left cheek banged against a hard stone. Shit, that stung. His eyes watered.

Carter let out an evil laugh and dug a hiking boot into his back as he stepped over him to catch Amanda.

"Son of a bitch." Jackson felt his eye. The skin below was puffing up into a healthy bruise. He ran a hand over his spine. "I think I slipped a disk, you fat-ass."

Carter climbed up the hill. "Jax, you're a pussy."

A pussy? Yeah, right. That came from the guy who has yet to beat me in a sport other than pool. Jackson pushed off the ground and lunged forward. It took four long steps to reach Carter. Jackson dove on Carter's back, wrapping him up in an old-fashioned football tackle. Both men went down with a thud, cavorting in a barrel roll.

"Hey!" They jolted around at the sound of Amanda's voice. She speared a finger at them—or just behind. "Look, you Neanderthals."

Jackson felt a cool breeze of air. He glanced over his shoulder. *Holy shit.* He was two inches from rolling off the path's edge, right into the tree tops ten feet below. Maybe not certain death but definitely serious injury-bound. "Oh, thanks."

Carter fisted Jackson's shirt and rolled his body to safety. Crawling to a knee, he gave a final shove to Jackson's chest and stood. "Grow up."

Jackson wanted to throw a retort but knew it would be equally juvenile to respond. He simply rose and dusted himself of debris while Carter joined Amanda, both leaving him standing like a ten-year-old caught playing in the mud before church. He wondered briefly where her friend Darlene had gone. Had she seen their wrestling match also?

Feeling chastised, he stood still and enjoyed the sun and scenery a moment before following. They crested the hill a few minutes later and took a different route to the bottom. Jackson pulled the map from his pocket, searching for a way to bypass them and win the challenge.

If he took the second trail to the left, he'd gain a quarter mile over the others. It looked steeper and he'd have to ford the water in the creek to beat them. *Wait.* The creek. Where Amanda *or* Carter would be skinny-dipping and soaking their tired legs if they won. He decided not to try to win the challenge after all. He grinned and hoped his timing would be impeccable.

The trees were shrouded in near-darkness when he finally reached an outcropping of rocks that smelled of damp moss and leaves. Eureka. Water spilled over the stones into a pool less than five feet below, then moved lazily down the river. The top of a head glistened, shiny and wet. From between the stones it was impossible to identify whether Carter or Amanda had won the bet but his money was on Carter. He seriously doubted anyone could outrun the former track star and health nut. Except himself, of course.

Jackson shucked his shorts and shirt, peeled off skivvies and shoes, and launched into a cannonball. He grabbed his knees, unworried about the water depth. They'd swam here as kids. It was safe. "Incoming!" His voice echoed off trees and hillside—along with the corresponding high-pitched scream.

Of Amanda's naked friend, Darlene. Shit.

Don't look, asshole. What an idiot idea.

When Jackson rose to the surface, he blinked twice and focused on the bank as he scrambled toward anonymity. Above he saw three sets of legs, two male and one female. Carter, the club organizer whose name escaped him, and Amanda.

"What the fuck, Jackson?" Carter frowned.

Darlene glided to the far side of the stream, then plunged behind an outcropping of granite that rose to make a great sunbathing ledge or hiding spot. She laughed. "Look, cowboy, as much as I like your company, give me a warning next time, okay? I'll skinny-dip with you any day but you scared the shit out of me."

Amanda plopped her hands on hips, chewing a wad of gum. Her eyes volleyed between Jackson and Darlene. Without a word, she threw her gaze toward the treetops and stomped away.

For more books by Shelley K. Wall, check out:

Text Me

Numbers Never Lie

Praise for *Numbers Never Lie:*

"Shelley K. Wall calculates a successfully suspenseful romantic tale with this digital page-turner. I loved the supporting characters as they added a fantastic depth to the story. I'm looking forward to seeing what else this author has to offer, and if it is half as interesting as this story it will be well worth picking up."—-Night Owl Reviews

"This was one of those reads that had it all: a heavy dose of suspense that kept me glued to the edge of my seat, enough action to make me want to scream out loud, and a lovely touch of mystery and romance.…Think John Grisham meets romance with a twist, with a touch of *Mission Impossible!*"—Harlequin Junkie

"Corporate shenanigans, betrayal and a happy-ever-after are all highlighted in this exciting thriller by Wall. Additionally, there's enough technical jargon to give credence to the story without overwhelming the reader."—RT Book Reviews

Bring It On

Praise for *Bring It On*

"*Bring It On* by Shelley K. Wall is a romance full of excitement and intrigue that will keep you turning the pages. If you want a fun, sexy, and intriguing read, then this book is for you."—Harlequin Junkie

"Wall's writing has the ability to grasp readers' attention . . . Hang on till the end—it's quite a surprise."—RT Book Reviews

The Designated Drivers' Club

Praise for The Designated Drivers' Club:

"Wall's latest will tug at your heartstrings with an emotional story of coping with death, managing family, and accepting love when it's being freely given. With situations that every reader can identify with—especially the difficulties of handling new love—this is easily read in one sitting."—RT Book Reviews

In the mood for more Crimson Romance?
Check out *Southern Hospitality by Amie Louellen* at
CrimsonRomance.com.